# CATFANG

'*Those Starstormers . . . The Emperor wants them and the Emperor will have them . . . They will be our breeding stock for the future.*'

Driven away from Epsilon Cool by the threats of the Octopus Emperor, the Starstormers are fugitives again, alone in the endlessness of space.

Then one day Vawn finds a stowaway on board – a scrawny, whining kitten. They name him Fang and he is a welcome distraction when the attacks begin.

Screaming projectiles batter the crazy homemade spaceship. The attacks intensify. Can *Starstormer* hold out? Fang, teeth bared, joins the battle . . .

*This is the third story in the Starstormer Saga*

# Catfang

Nicholas Fisk

KNIGHT BOOKS
Hodder and Stoughton

Copyright © Nicholas Fisk 1981

*First published by Knight Books 1981*

ISBN 0 340 26529 9

———————————————

Printed and bound in Great Britain for Hodder and Stoughton Paperbacks, a division of Hodder and Stoughton Ltd., Mill Road, Dunton Green, Sevenoaks, Kent (Editorial Office: 47 Bedford Square, London, WC1 3DP) by Hunt Barnard Printing Ltd., Aylesbury, Bucks.

# WHAT'S HAPPENED SO FAR

*Makenzi and Ispex; Vawn and Tsu. Two boys, two girls, of the next century. Left-behind children whose parents were building an exciting new world on a distant planet, Epsilon Cool. Dissatisfied children who hated their boring life in a run-down boarding school on Earth.*

*They wanted only to escape Earth and join their parents.*

*How? 'Build a spaceship,' said Makenzi. He meant it as a joke. But the joke became a plan and the plan a reality. For the hull, they hollowed out a meteorite. For the drives and equipment, they visited scrapyards and junk-heaps. For the crew, they had themselves – and an out-dated robot-computer whom they rightly named Shambles.*

*Amazingly, the ship was completed. They gave her the grand title of* Starstormer. *They themselves became the Starstormers. They crossed their fingers, pushed buttons, gritted their teeth – and blasted off into space!*

*They headed for the little planet of Epsilon Cool, on which their parents were preparing an Earthstyle settlement. This would be their home – or so they hoped. But first came the encounter with the great ship* Conqueror, *peopled by ageing humans and dominated by a Captain and officers who seemed to be regarded almost as priests ... priests of a religion whose sign was a figure of eight. But that sign, as the Starstormers knew, was the symbol of the Octopus Emperor – the legendary master of Tyrannopolis, the world of dark dust. Soon they learned that the Emperor was no legend. They witnessed the appalling*

5

*death of* Conqueror – *and realised that the Emperor truly existed. More: he was their enemy and their hunter.* (*Read* STARSTORMERS 1).

*Briefly, the Starstormers joined their parents. But soon the Emperor drove them back to their crazy little ship and the wilderness of space. They found another great Earthstyle ship with not a soul aboard. They discovered the terrifying purpose and destination of this ship – and discovered too that they were locked to it, unable to escape, as it accelerated to its doom.* (SUNBURST, Starstormers 2).

*A fluke saved them. The very power that doomed them proved to be their salvation. The danger over, they once again set course for Epsilon Cool and happiness. The happiness did not last. The Emperor of Tyrannopolis wanted human bodies, human skills . . .*

*So once more the Starstormers said farewell to the people and place they loved most. Once more they headed for nowhere and nothing.*

*Nothing, except adventure!*

# EMPTY SPACE

'*Death trap!*' Makenzi shouted, loudly and suddenly. The long, gloomy silence was shattered. Ispex blinked at Makenzi through his big spectacles. Vawn's nose and pale eyes appeared from behind the cloudy wings of hair hiding her face. Tsu, expressionless, raised one black eyebrow very slightly.

'*Death trap!*' Makenzi shouted again, furiously waving his long-fingered black hands. 'Here we are, in this crazy old rattletrap! – hurtling through space! – can't even hold a course! – and the Aircon's all over the place, one minute we're getting too much air, the next minute not enough! – '

'It's only the metering,' Ispex pointed out, mildly. 'I mean, the valves get jumpy . . . But it all evens out in the end. We're still *breathing*, aren't we?'

'*Starstormers*,' Makenzi said, bitterly. 'Us. Starstormers. Lunatics, more like. Morons. Imbeciles. Crazy old ship, load of junk – '

'You're bored,' Tsu said, flatly. 'The Aircon's working well enough, you know that. If it wasn't, you wouldn't be able to yell and shout and make a fuss, Makenzi.'

'Who's making a fuss?' Makenzi said. 'I'm merely pointing out that we'll all die in agony, gasping for breath and turning purple.' He pretended to choke himself, tongue out and eyes rolling.

'Actually, asphyxiation doesn't happen quite like that,' Ispex said, glinting his spectacles earnestly. 'What *really* happens is that – '

'Oh, shut up,' Makenzi said, gloomy again. He kept his back turned to the others and stared at Shambles, the robot, who flickered his lights uneasily. He knew he was being looked at. 'You're junk, too!' Makenzi told Shambles. 'Just like the ship! Just like everything!'

The robot began to stutter, 'P-p-pardon.'

Vawn told Makenzi, 'Don't take your stupid temper out on Shambles. All right, you're upset; we're all upset. We all miss our parents . . . ' Her voice faded. She lowered her head. The curtains of hair came down to hide her face. 'Oh dear,' she said. 'Oh, dear . . . ' She began crying.

It was Makenzi who laid a comforting hand on her shoulder. He did not say anything. There was nothing to say. All four of them suffered the same sense of loss, the same dull ache. They were parted from their parents, the only people they loved. They were fugitives in space once again, people on the run, escapers.

*Starstormer*, their spacecraft, was the vehicle of their escape. Yet it was also their prison.

What was to be done about it? Nothing. You kept your thoughts to yourself and did all the things that kept *Starstormer* habitable, flying and safe. If not safe, at least not *too* dangerous.

Vawn's smothered sobs died down. Soon there

8

was silence. Each of the four thought private thoughts.

Tsu thought about Vawn and the muffled sound of Vawn's sobbing in the night. Why was she crying? Because she wanted her parents: she wanted to be back on Epsilon Cool, the planet from which they had just been driven: back with the people who loved and protected her. So Vawn cried in the night and Tsu pretended not to hear.

Vawn thought about Tsu. Although the two shared a cramped little room (if you could call it a room, it was more like a cell carved out of grey-black rock) Vawn still knew next to nothing about Tsu.

Once, Tsu could have been the enemy, the traitor. In those days, Vawn had tried to read Tsu's isolated, oriental, golden, face. She had failed. When Tsu's parents, the captive slaves of Tyrannopolis, had been discovered and had died in their escape from slavery, Tsu's secrets had been revealed. Now Tsu became a heroine, a tragic heroine – but still her face told little or nothing and still her high, rattling, bossy voice could scrape Vawn's nerves.

Yet if anyone had a right to cry in the night, Tsu had. But she didn't cry. She slept, and the dim light in the tiny cell showed a sleeping face that could have been a mask. 'Leave me alone,' the face said, sleeping or waking. 'Leave me alone, I can manage on my own.'

Vawn sighed. 'Stop picking at yourself,' she told herself. 'Leave your fingernails alone. What would Mother say if she could see you . . . ' Just

9

thinking the word 'mother' made her throat begin to choke. So Vawn made herself look sideways out of her mane of hair. She looked at Makenzi. What was he thinking?

He was sulking: having a fit of gloomy temper. Well, why not? All the things he and the rest of the Starstormers wanted most – a place to live, people to love – were on Epsilon Cool. Every moment that passed took them further from Epsilon Cool.

And Ispex? His lower lip stuck out, his 'eye-specs', his spectacles, glinted. The eyes behind the lenses looked at nothing in particular and didn't see it. His shoulders were hunched and his pale, podgy hands fiddled idly with each other.

Vawn made herself get to her feet, briskly. 'I'm going to make drinks,' she said. 'Who wants what?'

There were mumbled replies.

Vawn said, 'All right, sulk. Have a really good sulk and leave me to do the work.' She strode away. Ispex said, 'S'pose I ought to help her,' but didn't get up. No-one else spoke or moved.

*Starstormer*'s galley or kitchen was near the centre of the snailshell-shaped ship, beside the fuels, drives and other services. Vawn therefore had to walk through a spiral corridor, with her head down to avoid hitting the low ceiling. As she walked, her nose wrinkled and twitched.

There was a smell.

'Something rotten,' she murmured. 'Food?' But the smell was not like that. It was faint but disgusting.

She went into the galley and sniffed. The smell was not so bad. She sniffed again. Hardly any smell. She shrugged and selected the chilly plasticans of drinks and put them on a tray. At the door of the galley, she paused. The smell again. She put down the tray and went to investigate.

She found the cause of the smell crouched behind a big fuel cell, right in the middle of the ship.

The cause was tousled, spiky, wet, filthy. It had white teeth and mewed.

It was a kitten.

# STOWAWAY

She forgot the drinks and attended to the kitten. She washed its scrawny little body. When she was finished her hands were bleeding where the kitten's claws and teeth had attacked her.

'*Bo, oful*,' she murmured.

Her eyes glazed with ecstasy, she took the kitten to the Starstormers. They gaped at it.

They put the kitten on a table and stared. It stared back, then spat.

Makenzi poked his hand at it. The kitten clawed and drew blood.

Tsu said, 'Good kitty-kitty, good little cat!' and carefully stretched out her hand. The kitten leapt sideways, bristled, and snarled 'Mrrraow!' Tsu pulled a face.

'You're gorgeous!' Vawn said, still in her trance. 'You booful little darling!' The expression on her face was of doting soppiness. The others stared at her in amazement. Ispex said, blankly, 'But he's awful! I mean, just look at him!'

They looked at him. He was the brindled kitten of the litter they had admired on Epsilon Cool. His coat was various shades of grey between black and white. His muzzle and whiskers and two front paws were white and his eyes yellow or green, according to the light. His ears and the tip of his tail were almost black. His damp fur was still stuck together in tufts. His ribs stuck out and the feet were too big for the bony legs.

'Oh,' Vawn mooed, 'I could just hug you to death!'

'Bet you couldn't,' Ispex said. 'Try it and he'd tear your eyes out!'

'He needs *foooooood*,' said Vawn, making the word a sickly lullaby.

'He needs drowning,' Ispex said.

Vawn ran back to the galley and returned with food packets. 'You can't give him that!' Makenzi said. 'That's our *real meat*! Our treat! He's not having that!'

Vawn ignored him. 'Who's a hungry ickle kitty, den?' she said, and, with bleeding fingers, gave the cat a large piece of real meat. Ice-cold as it was, the cat seized it with both front paws and attacked it savagely with its little white pointed teeth. It made horrible growling chewy noises and stared defiantly at the Starstormers.

Makenzi watched with disgusted horror. 'He'd eat *me*!' he said.

The kitten gulped down the last of the meat; hiccupped; opened its mouth incredibly wide; and said 'MRRRAOW!' It wanted more.

Ispex said, 'That cat is des-pic-able!' and walked out. Tsu went with him. Makenzi was already gone.

Vawn, eyes misty with loving tears, fed it.

\* \* \*

The kitten's hours and days passed in a sort of pattern.

When the kitten slept – and it slept a lot – Makenzi said, 'We've got to name him. You're sure it's a him?'

'He's a he,' said Vawn. 'I'm never wrong.'

'Well, he's got to have a proper name. None of your "Pussies" and "Toms" and "Tiddles". A real, proper name. Right then. Suggestions?'

'Boofuls,' said Vawn, dreamily. Everyone groaned. 'Starcat.' 'Silver.' 'Epsilon.' They argued so loudly about the names that the kitten woke up and said, 'Mrrrps!' – the sound it made when it wanted food. It often wanted food.

It finished the food and started licking Shambles. The robot said, 'P-pardon,' and moved away uneasily. The kitten again said 'Mrrrps!' and tried to bite one of Shambles' feelers.

'He'd eat anything,' Ispex said admiringly. 'He had a go at the soap the other day.'

'And the wrappings from the meat,' Makenzi said. 'In the end, he had to spit it out. But,' he added admiringly, 'he *tried* . . .'

Shambles, meanwhile, hid in a corner. The cat embarrassed him.

The kitten stared from face to face and repeated its hunger word, 'Mrrrps.' Nobody did anything. So it opened its jaws to their full extent, and gave a pathetic, strangled yowl.

'Booful teeth,' said Vawn.

'Row upon row of them,' Ispex said. 'Like a shark. Greedy devil.'

'You're not like a shark, are you, darlin'?' Vawn cried. And indeed the kitten was not. Its sleep and food had made it fluffier, prettier. With its mouth open and its shining eyes half closed and its tail shaking with impatience and greed, it was no longer repulsive. It had become just a hungry kitten.

It was Tsu who hit on the right name. She laughed at the furious kitten and said, 'You're so greedy. All mouth and teeth. I know what we ought to call you: Fang! Come here, Fang!' As if it recognised its new name, the cat ran to her.

'Fang . . . ' said Tsu, rubbing her cheek against the soft fur.

'Fang . . . '

\*     \*     \*

Only two Earth days later, the kitten-cat had become the most important member of *Starstormer*'s crew.

Vawn doted on him. She used baby-talk ('Oo luvs his mummy best, den?') until the other Starstormers winced, bellowed or even threw things at her. She took no notice. She smirked, Fang smirked.

Makenzi was as bad as Vawn but in a different way. He adopted a man-to-man approach to the cat. He called it 'old chap' and 'old fellow' as if he and Fang were characters in some dreadful old school story from a previous century. Worse, he sometimes went into his Negro-Scottish act. 'Och aye the noo,' he'd say, 'd'ye fancy a wee dochan-doris – a wee sup o' meelk?' Even the cat seemed bored by this.

Tsu said little to the kitten. She did not dote or croon or assume funny voices. But she did know how to tickle it expertly. She would silently pat her lap and the cat would jump on to it, back arched and tail straight. Then she tickled it, and her face and the cat's grew broader and smugger. The other Starstormers silently hated her for her success.

Ispex loved Fang deeply: but he was also curious. He wanted to know how the cat was made, how it worked, what it could do. He fed the animal's 'talk' into Shambles and tried to analyse the sounds. He studied bones, muscles, nerve endings, teeth, tongue and ear movements. Solemnly, he told the little cat, 'You're a wonder. Mag-ni-fi-cent! King of the beasts, that's what you are!'

Makenzi, overhearing, said, 'Ferocious feline! Red of tooth and claw! Take on anyone, anything! Look at those eyes!' Although it was Ispex's turn to have Fang, Makenzi tickled the cat's tummy. The cat grabbed at his fingers, first gently, then excitedly; then the rear legs started paddling. The claws came out. Makenzi said 'Ouch! Ow!' and laughed, afraid to take his hand away.

'The speed . . . ' Ispex said, admiringly. 'And when he plays with his toy – the ping-pong ball on the string – he's so fast! His reflexes, his nerve system, his muscles . . . everything so fast –'

'If we could harness that energy – ouch! – we'd have the finest – Ispex, make him let go! – the

finest fighting machine the Galaxy's ever seen!'
Makenzi said.

He thought he was making a mild joke. Later,
he'd remember his words with feeling.

# ATTACK

On the day of the first attack, Fang slept, curled up in a flattened ball, a sort of fur bun. His chin was supported by the tip of his tail. His four paws had disappeared, hidden by the warm, furry depths of the bun shape, whose middle rose and fell rhythmically with his breathing.

The four Starstormers sometimes paused in what they were doing (which was nothing much) to comment on the sleeping animal. 'He can actually *snore*,' Vawn said, adoringly. 'Did you know that? *Snore*. I've heard him, little tiny weeny snores – '

'Oh, belt up!' Makenzi said – but lazily, not angrily. The cat had changed the feeling of *Starstormer*: had made it a friendlier place.

Fang sneezed in his sleep, shook his head and resettled himself.

At the same instant that Fang sneezed, Shambles twitched and lights ran along the metal flanks of his body. Then Shambles went 'Glink!' as his drives engaged and his body moved an inch or two, uncertainly. Tsu said, 'What is it, Shambles?'

The robot said, 'P-pardon. My error. I thought – ' He made another uncertain, questing movement. 'Glink, glink-glink.'

Makenzi said, 'I thought you were going to see to his drive trains, Tsu?'

Shambles said, 'Pardon.' Now his lights were

running wild and his metal whiskers were twitching, aimlessly. He made his way to Ispex, who said, 'What is it, Shambles? Speak up!' But all Shambles could say was 'P-pardon. P-pardon-dondondon . . . '

Vawn said, 'Oh dear!' in a strangled voice.

Tsu looked into Vawn's face. 'You've gone pale. What's wrong?'

Vawn said, 'Nothing. I thought for a minute that – But it couldn't be! Not out here! We're so far away from – '

Then something went SLAM against the side of *Starstormer*. And from nowhere and everywhere, there was a sudden scream, a bellowing howl, that was over as soon as it started.

The Starstormers were all on their feet now, staring at each other with shocked eyes. Fang had arched his back. The fur bristled.

Makenzi was the first to recover himself. 'Did you record that, Shambles?'

'Yes.'

'Play it back.'

The robot obeyed. The Starstormers heard a tinny reproduction of the sounds.

Vawn said, 'Something hit us! What? Space detritus?'

Ispex said, 'Not detritus: not just floating muck or bits of meteorite. Doppler effect.'

'Doppler?'

'The scream was a sort of meow. A high *me*, then a low *ow*. Whatever made the noise was something passing us, very fast, something driven by power. I've studied the sounds, I know – '

Shambles interrupted, 'It was a projectile of some sort,' he said. 'D-definitely.'

SLAM!

This time *Starstormer* shook with the blow. And this time there was a flash of light which lit the real-view windows. The Starstormers ran to the windows and looked out. 'Nothing from this one,' Makenzi muttered over his shoulder, 'See anything from your RV over there?'

'Come over,' said Tsu, her high voice less sharp than usual. 'See for yourself.'

Makenzi went to the RV window. Still visible in the blue-blackness of space was a trail: a curved, luminous line, bright in the darkness, but fading fast.

'Projectile,' Ispex said. 'Something with drives. That was a deliberate attack.'

'But who? What? Why?' Vawn demanded. And then, just as she had done earlier, she said, weakly, 'Oh dear!'

'Go on,' Makenzi said, grimly. 'Oh dear what?'

'Can't you smell it?' Vawn said. Her voice shook. 'Can't *any* of you smell it? Shambles can, even Fang can, at least I think he can –'

'Go *on*,' Makenzi said. And then – 'Hot metal. That's it, isn't it?'

Vawn nodded miserably. 'Hot metal. The smell of Tyrannopolis. It's all starting again. They're after us.'

Ispex, still peering out of an RV window, said, 'All right, they're after us. So what? It's no good just standing there snivelling. What did they hit us with just now? Was it a missile or a craft or something fired from a craft or what? Are they going to give us another dose? We've got to know the *facts*.'

Furiously, he began prodding at Shambles. Rivers of lights ran over Shambles' sides: readouts appeared, were cancelled, were replaced by more.

Tsu bit her lip and suddenly marched out, very fast and determined. '*Weapons*,' she said, over her shoulder. 'We're not just going to stand here and be shot at, are we?'

Makenzi stood at one RV window, Vawn at the other. They stared into the darkness till their eyes ached. Half an hour passed and there had been nothing to see.

At last Vawn said, 'It's over for now. The smell's gone. Beside – look at Fang.'

Makenzi looked. The little cat was curled up again and fast asleep.

# THE PARENTS

On Epsilon Cool, the little planet from which the
Starstormers had been forced to flee, they sat by
the radio: Makenzi's parents, Jass and Verona, he
tall and strong and black, she warmly brown; Meg
and Clyde, mother and father of Ispex, he sandy
and round like his son, she plump and pink and
worried; and Vawn's parents, Dexter and Sheila,
the father serious, capable and solid (yet biting his
lip) his wife, Sheila, somehow cloudy like her
daughter, constantly pushing back her hair and
turning from one face to another, looking for
answers.

They turned over the same old questions.
Sheila said, 'We can't even be sure where they're
heading. I mean, that ship of theirs, it's such a –
such a – ' words failed her.

'It's a shrimp in an ocean,' Dexter said, forcing
a smile. 'The waves take it this way and that. It
swims, of course – waggles itself about in the
surging water – but it's still only a shrimp.'

'Very poetical,' Jass said. He too made himself
smile. The six of them, usually so easy in each
other's company, were uneasy when they talked
about their children. There were too many
frightening thoughts in their minds.

Sheila said, 'Well, then . . . what's the latest from
the Navplan?' A display on the wall bloomed

with light. Within its glow, a brilliant worm appeared, adding a tiny bit to its own length as they watched. The worm traced the course that *Starstormer* followed since leaving Epsilon Cool: a drunken course, a course that was a bad joke.

'Shrimp in an ocean,' Clyde murmured. 'It's terrifying – Oh well, at least they're heading in the same general direction. Away. And they're safer away from us.' His wife Meg made a protesting noise. Clyde said, 'No, but they are, aren't they? Tyrannopolis wants them, Tyrannopolis can't reach them. Surely you see that?'

In a very small voice, Meg said, 'Oh yes. I see that. I just wish we could hear them ... get in touch with them ...'

Verona said, 'We're trying all the time, Meg. You know that. The radio's on autoscan now, but there's always so much noise out there.'

Meg said, miserably, 'I don't trust machines. *I* want to try.'

Nobody stopped her as she cancelled the autoscan with a sweep of her hand and began her own search through space. Like the rest of them, she was an expert on every piece of equipment on the Epsilon Cool settlement. There was no hesitation in her plump fingers as they jabbed and prodded.

And there was no comment when a flickering rod of light settled into a pattern precisely the same as that made by the autoscan. She and the machine had reached the same dead end.

'Machines!' Meg said – almost shouted. 'What's the good of them? If only we could – if only we could . . . *They're* not machines, they're our children . . . '

The awkward silence that followed was ended by Jass. 'I agree,' he said, his voice low and comforting. 'Machines are wonderful : machines are no good. The problems they solve are the beginning of problems they cause. Well, half the time, anyhow.'

Meg neither heard nor answered. Near to tears, she was almost spitefully jabbing and prodding at the radio, making the screens draw meaningless patterns.

Sheila said, very quietly, 'I hate machines. It was machines that spoiled Earth. Machines that tempted people to escape Earth. It was a machine that took our children from Earth and another machine, a machine in the shape of a whole planet, that caused them to fly from this place . . . which is only a collection of machines. Machines, machines, machines – '

Dexter said, 'Yes, you could put it that way. But then, on the other hand – '

Meg suddenly and violently said, '*Quiet, everyone. Quiet!* Clyde, help me.' At once he was at her side, working as quickly and surely as she. The room was filled with splattering, fizzings, howlings – the audio signals, the noises.

'They make no sense !' Jass said. 'Or perhaps a new sort of sense . . . Meg, what have we got ? The children – '

Hurriedly, under her breath, she said, 'Nothing to do with the children. Another frequency, no-

24

where near theirs. I don't know what it is, we've never seen traces like this! – '

The screen was showing definite patterns, vase-shaped patterns of green light. Patterns with shape and purpose.

And then the audio signals began to have meaning too: beneath the random howlings and fizzings, there were other notes, a harmony of three notes close together . . .

'I'm filtering,' Clyde said. 'A bit more – a little bit more – ' And now the three notes were clear and loud and on their own. They were frightening.

Jass said, 'Navplan . . . I'll try the scout.' He began scouting through space, probing the nothingness for something. Something solid.

He found it. 'Craft of some sort,' he said. 'Going like hell.'

Now everyone was busy and talking.

'Three of them.'

'One note for each. Listen.'

'Coming towards us, very fast. Very, very fast,' Jass said.

'Any code-ins or recognition signals?'

'Nothing. So whatever they are, they're not likely to be friendly!'

'Couldn't they be – just meteorites, something harmless?'

'Not a hope. Those notes mean power. The craft are powered. Try an analysis, Dexter. We can't hope for much from that machine, but – '

'Machines!' Meg said. 'It took a human to find them! Me!'

'It may take machines to keep them off,' Jass

replied. 'These.' Briefly, he pointed his fingers at three panel buttons. All were shades of red.

One was marked POW, the second GUN and the third NUC.

POW meant bombs of energy sent along beams.

GUN meant traditional, gun-type weapons – the settlement bristled with them.

The third, NUC, meant Nuclear. 'NUC: *Now, Utter Catastrophe*,' Jass muttered to himself. For that was the joke. You weren't allowed to use *nuc* unless utter catastrophe threatened: and if you did use it, there would be an utter catastrophe. The *nuc* had never been fired.

'Coming closer, and fast,' Verona said. 'Pointed at us. No mistake about it.'

'How long before they arrive?' Jass said.

'Two minutes,' Verona replied.

'Sheila: weapon check.'

She checked the weapons. She pressed one cluster of buttons twice, then a third time. Her face was shocked. 'We've three *pows* missing,' she said.

'But that's impossible!'

'Impossible or not, they're missing.'

'But – but –'

'Never mind the buts,' Sheila said. 'Are we going to be attacked? What do we do?'

Jass said, 'A minute. We've got about a minute. If they attack, we've got all the weaponry we need. But will it do us any good? What do you think, Dexter?'

'Depends what they're after. If they want to hit *us*, they're probably out of luck. We should get them first. But if they want to damage the *settlement* – '

He shrugged. In his mind's eye, he could see their home settlement on Epsilon Cool. From space, it looked like the joined-together bubbles you see when you wash up. Under the biggest bubble was the settlement itself, and the people in it. The other, linked bubbles were there to hold in an atmosphere that humans could breathe – that plants could grow in, one day – that humans and their animals could thrive in.

The bubbles were very delicate.

'Ten seconds,' Verona said. 'Arm and aim, OK?'

'Armed and aimed on *gun*.'

'OK on *pow*, manual and auto.'

'Listen!' A distant screaming, fast coming closer.

'Fire *gun* to miss. Repeat, *miss*.'

'Fired and missed, OK.'

Now they could hear, with their own ears, the scream and bellow of three craft. The three notes became one note, a note that corkscrewed into the brain, making eyes flinch and teeth grit.

Then a physical shock, a blow that shook and battered, as the three craft hurtled over and away; and the explosions of the *gun* missiles, aimed to miss.

And then the voice: the Voice of Tyrannopolis.

# THE THREAT

'Thank you for firing to miss,' the Voice said. 'Nice of you.'

'How did they know – ' Sheila began, but then remembered the dust that had long ago invaded the settlement: the dust that listened and heard and told every secret to the Emperor of Tyrannopolis.

'All right,' Jass said. 'What's it about? Are you attacking us? Come closer and we'll shoot you down.'

'If you were stupid enough to put out of control just one of those craft,' the Voice said, 'it could rip your settlement from end to end like gutting a rabbit. Is that a good Earthstyle phrase? It would tear through those bubbles of yours – '

'Get *on*,' said Jass. 'What do you want? What's it all about?'

'It's about two things,' said the Voice. 'First, our experiments in Earthstyle hardware. Thanks to the skills and hands of those humans who are our guests – the ones you call our captives, or slaves, though they returned here of their own free will – thanks to them, we have now completed a number of destroyer craft. Destroyers . . . sounds old-fashioned doesn't it? But they aren't old-fashioned.'

'And second?' Jass growled.

'Second, those children of yours. Those Star-stormers. Funny name, but sad, too. I told you once before that the Emperor wants them – '

'The Emperor betrayed us,' Dexter shouted. 'He broke his word.'

'The Emperor wants them and the Emperor will have them,' the Voice said. 'You must understand how important your children are to us. They will be our breeding stock for the future. You humans don't last very long, you know. You wear out too quickly: and the old ones don't remain efficient. Our present human stock is running out. There have been *deaths*.' The voice sounded annoyed. 'Too many have died recently. We must have new, young, hands, eyes, skills. Now and for the future. So please instruct your children to return. The Emperor needs them. The Emperor will have them.'

'We can't instruct them. We can't reach them, surely you know that. There's no radio link between us and them – '

'And we have no intention of *instructing* them,' Meg said, her voice shaking with fury. 'Do you really think we'd tell our children to become slaves of your Emperor! – '

'You'd better,' said the Voice, blankly. 'You'll make contact eventually. You'd better make them obey.'

'And if we don't?' Jass said at last.

The Voice said, 'Our destroyers are designed to destroy.'

'Look,' Jass said, 'Wait a minute – '

'Obey and your children live. Disobey, and that

little meteorite thing of theirs – that *Starstormer* –
will be reduced to its original condition: junk. A
bright dot in the sky for a second or two, then
little bits of junk, little rags of flesh and bone.'

'You'll get nothing from us,' Clyde said.
'Certainly not our children!'

'Oh yes we will,' said the Voice. It sounded very
pleased with itself. 'We'll get your children. One
way or another. Think about it. But don't talk too
loudly. We can hear you, remember.'

Suddenly the speakers were silent. The six
people who had been listening to it stared at the
ground. At last, Jass said, '*Do* we tell the children?'

'Are you mad?' Verona said. 'Of course not!
Haven't they got enough to worry about? –'

'Besides, what could they *do*?' Sheila said. 'How
can they protect themselves?'

'Say nothing,' Dexter said.

Jass shrugged. 'You're right, of course,' he
said, bleakly. 'Say nothing.'

# POW

'Weapons,' Tsu said – and threw three dull, black, heavy tubes on the floor.

The others stared wide-eyed at the tubes then at Tsu. Makenzi, the whites of his eyes enormous against the blackness of his face, said, 'But! – but! – but! –'

Tsu said, 'Not but-but-but. Pow-pow-pow. You look like frogs, you lot. Goggling. These are *pows*: p.o.w.s. *Pow* guns. I stole them when we were on Epsilon Cool. While you lot were messing about in the pool.' She stared coolly from face to face, daring anyone to challenge her.

The three *pows* glinted dully on the floor, challenging nothing and no-one. They were just metal objects.

But as everyone knew, a *pow* could take on almost anything. They fired bombs consisting of pure energy: bombs that formed and exploded only when the carrying beams were on target. A correctly aimed carrier beam bounced back, when it found a target, into the muzzle of the *pow*. The *pow* then delivered a bomb of power sufficient to drill a hole through a small mountain. The whole process – beam, bounce, bomb – took millionths of a second.

'But they're *illegal*,' Makenzi said. 'I mean, only the Galactic Authority issues *pows* –'

'I issued these,' Tsu said. She kicked one of the tubes with her toe.

'But you took them from Epsilon Cool – from our parents! You'll get them into trouble, terrible trouble!' Vawn cried. 'First, because they've let the weapons get into the wrong hands –'

'Nothing wrong with my hands,' Tsu said, showing her clean, neat, golden hands.

'And second because you've taken away their defence. They need the *pows* to defend themselves –'

'You think we don't?' Tsu said: and imitated the slam and scream of whatever it was that had hit *Starstormer*. Then she said, 'They've got ten *pows* on Epsilon Cool. I took three. So they've still got seven. Fair shares.'

Amazingly, Ispex began to laugh. He laughed and laughed until Makenzi hit him hard on the back and shouted, 'What's so funny? Tell us! *Tell* us!'

'She's got the *pow*,' Ispex choked, 'But she's forgotten the *er*! Her *er*'s missing! Where's her *er*?' He began giggling again.

Makenzi pushed him over sideways and looked up at Tsu, scowling. 'Well, is he right?' he asked her. 'Did you forget the *er*?'

'I don't understand –' Vawn began, but Tsu cut across her. 'Oh, I know what Ispex means,' she said. 'A *pow* is no good without power. Power. Very funny joke. Well, we'll just have to get the power, won't we? Won't we, Ispex? I mean, we don't have to use our drives all the time, do we? Do we, Ispex?'

Ispex stared at her. He said, 'You mean, if we had to fight – use the *pows* – we could cut the ship's drives and divert the power to the *pows*?'

'Why not?' Tsu said. 'If we've got enough energy to drive this ship umpteen thousand kilons an hour, haven't we got enough to make a *pow* go bang? All we have to do is switch it.'

'But *how*?' Ispex demanded. 'How do we make the link? With a bit of flex and a silver-paper fuse? How do we do it?'

'That's just what I was going to ask you,' Tsu said, her face expressionless and her voice high and cold. 'You're the brainy one. You've often told us so. And you've got Shambles to help you. And all kinds of gear lying around. So you adapt this and tinker with that –'

'How, *how*, HOW?' Ispex shouted.

Tsu shrugged and turned her back on him. 'Somebody ask me if I remembered to steal the mounts and aimers for the *pows*,' she said.

Makenzi, dry-voiced, said, 'Well, did you? Because without them, the *pows* are no good to us –'

'You'll find the mounts and aimers hidden near the ion drive set-up,' she said. 'Let's go and get them and put everything together and get used to handling the *pows*. Because I think we're going to need them. Vawn's nose keeps twitching.'

Vawn nervously touched her nose. 'I don't smell anything *now*,' she said, uncertainly. 'No hot metal or anything. At least, I don't *think* there's anything . . . ' She jumped to her feet and said, 'Right or wrong, we've got the weapons. Let's do what Tsu says – get everything together.' She ran to the centre of the ship. The others followed.

Alone, Shambles clicked and hummed and ran rivulets of lights along his flanks. He was trying to find traces of the enemy; evidence of a coming attack.

There was nothing definite, and yet ... and yet ...

\* \* \*

On Epsilon Cool, Clyde, father of Ispex, reported to Jass, Makenzi's father. 'It's not possible,' Clyde said, 'but it's happened all the same. Three *pows* gone. Vanished. Someone broke into the armoury, got the stuff – mounts and aimers too – then re-coded the locks and left everything looking just as it was before.'

'When?' Jass said. 'What day did the thefts occur?'

Clyde said the date, Jass repeated it, then began to chuckle, very softly. 'The children were here then,' Jass said. 'The children have got those *pows*. I don't know how, but they did it! Which one, I wonder? Not your son Ispex. Not my Makenzi. No, it must have been that Chinese minx, that Tsu.' His chuckling became laughter. 'Remember how she got the meteorite from the junkyard – The meteorite that became the hull of *Starstormer*? Just imagine, she tricked a Boss unit to get that! Even got it delivered!'

'And now she's tricked another Boss,' Clyde said, soberly. 'She's tricked *you*. It could mean the end of your career, Jass. When this gets reported –'

34

'Reported?' Jass said. 'You mean, put on the official, monthly, Earthside report?'

'But of course! We send in reports every month, you know that. Hell, you *sign* them!'

'I sign anything you put in front of me, Clyde,' Jass said. 'Anything at all.'

Clyde bit his lip and said, 'It's the man who signs the report that bears the responsibility, Jass.'

'That's right,' Jass said. 'My responsibility.'

The two men were silent until Jass said, 'When did we last have an inspection, Clyde?'

'I don't remember. Yes I do. Two years ago, almost. But there could be another at any time.'

'Yes, any time,' Jass agreed. Then, 'Just imagine, Clyde, being out there with those kids in that horrible ship. Without any weapons.'

Clyde went on biting his lip. Then he gave a long sigh and said, 'Oh, well . . . Here's the report, Jass, up to date and ready for you to sign.'

Jass read through the document. It listed all the equipment, supplies and stores on Epsilon Cool. Under 'Armoury', it read, 'WEAPONS, *pow*. Supplied, 10. Held at present date, – –.'

'Why, Clyde!' Jass said, 'Look at this! You've left a blank here! Your report isn't complete!'

'Good heavens!' Clyde exclaimed. 'Mercy me!' He leaned across and wrote in the missing figure. Now the report read, 'WEAPONS, *pow*. Supplied, 10. Held at present date, 10.'

'That's better,' Jass said. '*Much* better.' Then he flipped to the last page of the report and signed his name with a bold signature in clear, steady handwriting.

# DEFENCE

The Starstormers waited for the next attack. It never came. 'But if it does,' Ispex said, 'We'll be ready . . .'

He pressed a *pow's* trigger. A violent lance shot from *Starstormer* and pierced the darkness. He pressed the second *pow's* trigger and – zippp! – the same thing happened, but the lance of light was at a different angle. '*Pow!*' Ispex murmured. 'Pow-pow-pow!' The lances flickered like the tongues of snakes. 'Just think what it will be like when we've got power behind those beams!' Ispex said happily.

'When will that be?' Vawn said.

'And how much power?' Makenzi asked.

'I don't know,' Ispex confessed. 'A lot. Well, quite a lot. Enough to make a big hole in that spacecraft that came to Epsilon Cool from Tyrannopolis. You know, when they picked up the slaves.'

'Therefore our *pows* might be some good?' Makenzi said.

'Yes,' Shambles said. 'That is, yes and no. That is – it all depends on –'

'Thank you very much, Shambles,' Makenzi said. 'Don't know what we'd do without you.'

Ispex said, 'I've got the mount properly fixed now for the third *pow*, and Tsu's trying to finish up the aimers. She says she's got them fast, but not accurate. We're trying a spinwheel sort of control, you run your fingers and thumbs over the little wheels to set your aim. I'm not sure . . . It's not a natural way to control anything, if you know what I mean . . .'

'Why not use Shambles?' Vawn said.

'He's not built for it. He's an analyser, not a quick-fire computer.'

'Wobble plate linked to a visual display,' Ispex said. 'That's what we need. I said so all along, you wouldn't listen – '

'We did listen, you didn't tell us how to fix the wobble plate. You didn't tell us because you don't know.'

'Well, it is complicated,' Ispex said. 'Better to have something ready now that definitely works, rather than something that – '

Shambles squawked: 'Attack! Attack!' and began flashing lights and read-outs.

Ispex said, 'Oh, shut up, Shambles, not *now*!' Shambles said, 'P-pardon,' and shut up.

'He enjoys our practice alerts,' Ispex explained. 'I programmed him to give me an alert at random times so that I learn to respond quickly, you see . . . I think he enjoys it, don't you, Shambles? But it's getting boring. I want to link up the *pows* to the power. That's the *real* job. At the moment, all we've got is an aiming system. But when I milk the power from our drive units – '

'Our ship will blow up?' Makenzi suggested.

Ispex considered the question carefully, frowning and pulling at his lower lip. At last he replied, 'Not *necessarily*.'

37

'Oh, good,' Makenzi said. 'Goody, goody, good. So our weapons won't necessarily kill us?'

Ispex gave Makenzi a dignified glare and went to the centre of the ship where the power was. The power was vast, and vastly dangerous. Allowed to run wild, it could destroy a city.

Lips pursed, Ispex began tinkering with silicon modules, armoured relays and all the other gadgets that were meant to contain, hold and channel the raging, devilish power. Sometimes the power, like a wild beast in a flimsy cage, would make a tigerish spring, trying to escape: then warning lights would flash, needles would jump and the wild beast might even snarl and flash and burn metal.

When these little accidents happened, Ispex nodded his head and said, 'Ah, I see . . . ' Then he tried something else.

He was perfectly happy.

# SECOND ATTACK

Three days passed and then, 'Attack!' Shambles squawked – and at the same instant, SLAM! and *Starstormer* jumped and juddered with the shock of the hit – and Vawn screamed, Makenzi toppled over, Tsu fell too but was on her feet again almost before she hit the floor –

KREE–OW! – and another slam from another ship –

Then panic as the Starstormers all shouted at once. 'Where's Fang, poor Fang?' Vawn hooted. 'Shambles! Why didn't you warn us?' shouted Makenzi. 'P-pardon, you instructed me not to – you accused me of f-false alarms –'

Tsu was making a sort of furious hissing noise, her narrow eyes made wide with anger and fear.

Shambles blurted and blundered and flashed lights.

'Where's poor darling Fang! –'

'Never mind Fang, this is serious –'

'P-pardon –'

'Get out of my way, get out of my way!' This was Ispex. He was pushing Makenzi and Vawn aside, pushing at Tsu's shoulders to guide her to the control panel that was supposed to fire the *pows*.

'You're too late,' Makenzi shouted. 'It's all over! You and your *pows* . . . Fat lot of use they are! –'

Another slam, another dying scream, proved Makenzi wrong. The attackers were back again.

Makenzi flung himself at Shambles and crouched by the robot, trying to take in the torrent of read-outs that raced along the robot's sides.

Vawn, still shouting, 'Fang!', ran to an RV window and stared out with wide, terrified eyes. She saw burning violet trails, scars in the darkness left by the attackers. She shouted to Makenzi but he had no time for her. He bellowed, 'Never mind the *pows*, Ispex, help me with Shambles!'

But Ispex and Tsu were at their action stations, Tsu with her small white teeth showing between her parted lips and Ispex looking old, an ancient professor, his plump, sandy face pinched by a furious pout of concentration, his fingers furiously turning the aimer's spinwheels.

'Attack!' Shambles yelped.

This time, Ispex, Tsu and the *pows* were ready.

'NOW!' shouted Ispex – and his fingers scurried over the spinwheels, stopping their spin. '*Now!*' – and Tsu, her face a mask of happy malice, prepared to stab three red buttons in quick succession. Now, all the power of *Starstormer* should be channelled into the three *pows*. Now, the aiming beams should flicker like rapiers – find the target – lock on it – then carry the vast bolts of raw power that blow apart the enemy, reduce it to white-hot flying fragments! . . .

'*Now!*' Her fingers jabbed down on the buttons. Her eyes blazed, her breath made a sharp, cat-

40

like hiss between her clenched teeth. The joints of her fingers whitened with pressure.

And nothing happened.

No blast of power to rock the ship. No locking beams of energy, no bolts of thundering power, no smashing explosions and whirling firestorms in the blackness outside –

Nothing but Fang. With a yell of outrage, the little cat, eyes ablaze and fur electrified, sprang from his hiding place under Tsu's control panel. 'MRRROW!' he shouted. His voice was both outraged and pathetic. His fur stuck out in spikes.

Vawn flung herself at him and cradled him in her arms. 'Did he get a nasty fright, then?' she moaned. 'Did nasty Tsu frighten poor Fangsy?'

Outside, the howl of the attacking craft died and was gone. Ispex stared at Vawn and the cat with cold loathing. Then he knelt down and burrowed under the firing panel. At last he surfaced, holding a piece of red wire, strangely crinkled and crimped.

'Your cat,' he told Vawn in a strangled voice, 'has been chewing our firing wiring.'

'The firing wiring?' Vawn said, blankly.

'The firing wiring,' said Tsu and Ispex, both at once, both furiously.

Makenzi was the first to laugh. Once started he could not stop. 'Firing wiring!' he said, clutching his knees and shaking with laughter. '*Firing wiring . . .*'

Tsu was the last to laugh. Ispex gave in early, rolling on the floor with Makenzi. 'Chewing firing wiring . . .'

Only Vawn did not laugh. 'Firing wiring could

be *bad* for him,' she complained, outraged.

In the blue-blackness outside, the trails made by the attackers finally faded and died. The attack was over. *Starstormer*, slowly spinning like a thrown rock, continued her voyage into the endless nowhere of space.

# CONTACT

'What's the damage?' Makenzi said, half an hour later. The laughter was over for all of them.

'Nothing much,' Tsu said. 'Whatever it was they fired at us, hit us. But it didn't do much harm, the outside TVs just show chips of meteorite off our hull.'

'What are they after?' Ispex said. 'I mean, why attack us and not destroy us? Why not do the job properly?'

Ispex muttered, '*What* are they? And *why*? And *when* will the next attack come? Tsu, I've got the wiring done, everything's OK now. Shall we run another test?'

'If you like,' Tsu said.

'I'm not so sure *I* like,' Makenzi said. 'If those *pows* of yours had worked, we might have been worse off than ever. Might have blown ourselves to smithereens. If we've got to be killed, I'd rather *they* did it than *we*. You and Tsu, messing about with things you don't understand . . .'

Ispex was just about to make a furious reply when the tinny voice of Shambles interrupted. 'Radio!' he said. 'Quiet, please! We're getting signals from Ep-ep-ep-ep –'

'*Epsilon Cool?*' cried the Starstormers. The *pow* argument was forgotten.

Yet it was the *pow* question that spoiled what

43

followed – the brief, fluke-ish conversation with Epsilon Cool and the parents, thousands and thousands of kilons away . . .

The distant words came through storms of interference: electronic cacklings, whistlings, blatterings, hootings, whines and screeches . . .

'Can you . . . us? We thought we heard you just now when . . . Send "receive", send an OK, tell us if . . . '

This was Epsilon Cool. Makenzi, hands trembling, coded Shambles. 'Say we're receiving,' he hissed, urgently. 'Tell them to keep sending.'

'Love . . . are you all right? Are you well? Are you . . . All our love . . . You were right to go, you had to . . . thinking of you all the . . . Vawn, mother's much better, she says she . . . Are you OK? Are you well?'

Makenzi said, 'Enough. Cut through. Send "All OK, all OK". Give it a ten-second repeat, then five seconds of "Over". Perhaps they'll come back clearer.' His voice was hoarse. He was sweating.

The interference suddenly cleared. For long minutes, the Starstormers spoke to their parents – spoke in clear words, whole sentences. Tsu, whose parents had died on Tyrannopolis, was not forgotten: Jass and Verona, Meg and Clyde, Sheila and Dexter, all spoke to her. As she replied, her sharp voice softened.

The conversation became practical. There was talk of food, power – and Tyrannopolis. The great ship that had carried away the slaves had not been seen again . . .

'Oh, never mind *them*,' Vawn shouted. 'Tell us about *you*, yourselves! And Epsilon Cool! And then I'll tell you about the kitten, Fang –'

The voices blundered into each other because of the time lag between saying and hearing. Now Vawn's father, Dexter, was talking about Epsilon Cool. 'Big excitement about a robbery,' he said. 'Just about the time you left. When you come back, we'll have to talk about it. Have a pow-wow. A *pow-wow*. Are you receiving? Did you hear? Over.'

The Starstormers stared at each other. Vawn said, 'What does he mean? I don't get –'

Makenzi said, 'Oh, don't be so dim,' and Ispex said, 'A *pow*-wow, stupid. He's asking us about the *pows*. He can't say it in plain words, because there's a chance that he'll be heard Earthside. Makenzi, what do we say?'

'Nothing.'

'We've got to say something, they're our parents, we could get them into trouble.'

Tsu made up their minds for them. 'Yes,' she said into the microphone, 'Yes. *Pow*-wow. Yes, we hold *pow*-wow. The answer is Yes. Over.'

'Tell them we're sorry,' Makenzi said. 'Tell them to blame us if there's trouble. Tell them –'

But it was too late. The interference rolled back. smothering the fragile radio waves. The voices were gone.

The Starstormers, silent, separately, remembered the treasured words the waves had carried. And Shambles edited the tape he carried, knowing it would be wanted for replay. Again and again.

\* \* \*

45

'The attacks!' Tsu said a little later. 'Not one of us mentioned them! We must have been mad! We didn't tell them a thing! –'

'So we didn't,' said Ispex, calmly.

'Quite forgot,' Vawn said.

'Lapse of memory,' Makenzi said, smugly.

Tsu stared from face to face. 'But *why*?' she said. 'I mean, they might have been able to tell us things! Help us fight off the attacks! So why –'

Makenzi stretched and sighed. 'Look, Tsu,' he said, 'What's the point of telling them? I mean, how would you feel if *you* were a parent and it was *your* children . . .'

'And what would you do?' Makenzi went on. 'Actually *do*? To help them?'

'Nothing,' Tsu admitted. Then she said, 'I see what you mean.'

'Fight our own battles,' Ispex said, dourly. 'Win or lose, they can't help us. No good running to mummy and daddy.' After a pause, he said, 'I've got plans for a wobble-plate controller. I don't like these spinwheels, too slow.'

Tsu looked from face to face before she spoke. She straightened her shoulders. 'I don't mind us being on our own. In fact, I like it. After all – ' she threw back her head, raised her arms high – 'we are the Starstormers!'

'Good old us!' Makenzi shouted, and stood on his head.

a cautious paw. It didn't do anything. He sniffed it. It didn't smell of anything. He explored it with the tip of his nose. It didn't feel as if it might produce a sting, or nippers, or claws.

So he opened his mouth and swallowed it.

Then he curled himself up under the console, folded his front paws under his chest and prepared to sleep.

\*　　\*　　\*

Before Fang could fall asleep, however, footsteps came running: Tsu and Makenzi. Makenzi ran to Shambles, put him back on his wheels the right way up and shouted, 'What do you mean? What attack? Who's attacking us?'

'It was *me*,' Shambles said, shakily. 'It was *I*. That cat Fang attacked me! That cat Fang – catfangcatfangcatfang – ' His voice let him down. Makenzi had to press his cancel button three times before he could get Shambles properly restarted and hear the whole story. 'Is *that* all,' he said disgustedly when Shambles had finished.

Vawn arrived in time to hear the last of the tale. 'Oh, poor Fang!' she hooted. 'My darling, my own! Come to mother, den!' She cradled the cat and crooned over it. It burped gently at her. 'Oh, poor precious darling,' cried Vawn, 'He's got that terrible thing inside him, he'll die!'

'No he won't,' said Makenzi sourly. 'If it disagrees with him, he'll make a disgusting mess somewhere when he sicks it up. I'll bet it's me that has to clear up the mess.'

Vawn did not hear his words, of course. 'Oh, poooor Fang,' she cried. 'Who knows what it will do to him? Anything might happen!'

What did happen was something stranger and more important than she, or any of the other Starstormers, could ever have imagined . . .

# FAILURE

The third attack happened in the middle of what the Starstormers called night – that is, the time when they slept.

It took even Vawn by surprise. She smelled nothing because she was asleep, like the others. But she was awake, instantly, when her bed and the whole ship shook; when once again there was that terrifying SLAM! as *Starstormer* took the blow directed by the attacking craft that screamed and howled outside; when the smell of hot metal crept into her nostrils.

'Attack! Attack!' shouted Shambles. 'I know, I know,' Ispex mumbled as he rushed from the warmth of his bed to the *pow* controls. 'Tsu!' he shouted. 'Quick! Action stations!'

She was there already, her face set and her fingers poised over the firing buttons. 'This time,' Ispex said, '*this* time . . .!' She nodded at him. This time there would be no mistake. This time, the *pows* would fire and the attacking ships would burst and blaze and shatter –

SLAM! Ispex was almost knocked sideways, but even as he fell he somehow tripped the spinwheels just at the very moment when they were dead on. Outside *Starstormer*, the luminous beams followed the attacking craft – converged on one of them, held it in a triangular crisscross, followed it – and the red light shone on Tsu's console –

'FIRE!' he shouted, but of course her fingers had already descended on the buttons.

*Starstormer* bucked like a horse stung by a hornet. All the power the ship had was suddenly diverted to the tubes of the *pows*, and from them along the violet beams leading to the attacking craft.

The power formed a bombshell. The bombshell exploded.

'Hit!' Ispex whooped. 'Hit, hit, hit!' He ran to the nearest RV window to see with his own eyes the destruction of the enemy craft. Tsu joined him, her face alight with furious joy.

In the darkness, a puffy cloud of energy, violet energy, pulsed and shimmered, changing shape jerkily, leaking flashes of coloured fire, shimmering and wobbling, always expanding.

'It worked! It worked!' Ispex shouted in Tsu's ears. She was shouting too, hugging herself and yelling, 'Hit! Hit! Hit!'

Shambles' squawk said, 'Miss.'

Stunned, Tsu and Ispex turned to the robot. 'But it must have been a hit,' she said. 'The *pows* can't explode if the aiming's wrong!'

'Three craft in the attack,' said Shambles. 'Three craft still out there. Wait. I am plotting the course of the craft and also the shots you fired. Wait . . . There! You see? Look at the screens.'

The screens recorded what had happened all too clearly. The three attackers showed as smooth, looping curves: the *pows* as absolutely straight lines, needle-fine.

The lines converged – and met – and made a lingering glow on the screens.

The Starstormers stared dully at each other.

'Failure,' said Ispex. 'Doesn't work. Stupid, useless . . . !' He kicked the aiming console savagely, hurting himself but not the metal and plastic. 'Why? *Why?*'

'Worse still,' Tsu said, 'how did we get *pows* exploding when they weren't on target? I mean, that's impossible, it just can't happen!'

'A *pow* hit a *pow*,' Shambles said, his voice flatter than ever.

'*What?* You mean we aimed and fired at our own beam?'

'I am sorry, but yes. That is what I mean. Your aiming system is un-unsatisfactory. It cannot distinguish friend from foe. Also, it is too slow. Also, it is incapable of improvement. Also – '

Makenzi and Vawn came in. Vawn said, 'The attack seems to be over. What happened?'

'Aiming system failed,' Ispex said. 'It will always fail. I've been thinking – '

'Think fast,' Makenzi said. 'Next time we'll all be dead.'

'That's right, all dead,' Ispex said – and started rubbing his forehead. 'I must think. *Think*. Because of the present system's failure – '

From nowhere, a voice seemed to echo his words. 'Failure . . . ' it said, indistinctly. '*Failure* . . . '

'Who said that? Who spoke?' Makenzi demanded.

The voice, very faint and blurred, spoke again. '*Failure* . . . ' it said.

55

Vawn stared wildly at the others. 'I didn't speak. Did you? Or you?'

Ispex said, 'No, perhaps it was Shambles?'

'P-pardon, no.'

'*Failure*,' said the faceless, mouthless voice.

Then, very quietly, it began to laugh.

# THE VOICE

It was Fang who found the source of the voice.

While the Starstormers stared at each other in wonder, the little cat twitched his nostrils, laid back his ears, and glared. Stiff-legged, he prowled the room.

'*Failure*,' said the ghost voice, clear now, no longer muffled and blurred.

Fang thrust his head forward, mouth snarling and quivering: then jerked it back again, as if he had tasted something bad.

'You were talking of failure,' said the voice. Now it was crystal clear. The Starstormers recognised it.

'Tyrannopolis,' Vawn said, and shuddered. 'The Voice of Tyrannopolis!'

Makenzi quietened her with a wave of his hand.

'You and your failures!' said the Voice. 'You always sound so surprised by them! We are never surprised. We are surprised only by your successes! The four of you, in that insane ship of yours. The four of you hurtling blindly through space, running away from you don't know what, rushing towards nothing in particular . . . '

The Voice laughed. The laughter was soft and self-satisfied.

'Why do you do it?' the Voice continued. 'Why do you bother? What do you hope for? Escape?

Escape from what? From the Emperor of Tyran-nopolis? But he is your friend! He is waiting to welcome you, to help you!'

Now Fang's back was arched. His mouth was open, the tiny white teeth showed. His eyes were focused on something the Starstormers could not see.

'. . . And your parents,' said the Voice. 'Why did you leave them? Why leave the people you love the most – the people who love you the most?'

'Shut up about our parents!' Vawn shouted wildly. Her clumsy hands flailed furiously at nothingness. 'Shut up, shut UP!' Again Makenzi restrained her.

'If only you would listen,' said the Voice. 'Listen to the voice of reason. *My* voice. If only you would attempt to understand! But, no. You blunder off into space – lurch away in a blind panic, heading for inevitable disaster, inevitable suffering –'

Fang leapt. He sprang at nothing, front legs splayed outward, claws spread. The claws tore at nothing, rending and tearing.

And suddenly the Voice was silent, and Fang was sniffing daintily at something on the floor, something that nobody could clearly see: a patch of shadow that moved, scuttling sideways –

'*Dust!*' Vawn said. She was kneeling by Fang, her hand on his neck, staring, like him, at the ground. She looked up at the others, her eyes wide. 'I'm sure I saw it,' she cried. 'Dust. But now it's gone.'

As if to prove her words, Fang sniffed the ground

and tried to follow invisible tracks that led him nowhere. At last he looked up at Vawn, obviously puzzled, and said, 'Mrr-aow?'

'He saw it too,' Vawn said. 'He saw it first, when we couldn't see anything – '

'You're right,' Ispex said. 'He saw it. He got rid of it. We couldn't see it but he could.' He bent down and picked up Fang, tickling the cat's furry neck. 'Clever old Fang,' Ispex said. The cat blinked and pushed its head against Ispex's finger.

Then Tsu spoke. 'But what did he see?' she demanded. 'What did he get rid of?'

But of course there was no answer. Not at first.

# INSIDE FANG

'What they did,' Ispex said, when the Starstormers held a Council of War to discuss the latest attack, 'was to build a sort of radio, right here in this ship. This room.' His lower lip stuck out. He pulled at it with finger and thumb. His spectacles glinted.

'By "they", you mean Tyrannopolis?' Vawn said absently, stroking Fang.

The others groaned. 'Who else?' Makenzi said, loudly. 'Wake up, Vawn!'

'But they couldn't have done that,' Vawn said, smugly. She was concentrating on Fang, not the conversation. 'Radios have to have transistors and wires and things. All sorts of things. Did oo love oo muvver, den?'

More groans. Even Fang turned his back on Vawn and began cleaning the fur on his tail, his body twisted in a complicated knot centred on his stomach. In the middle of his vigorous cleaning, he burped loudly -- sat up straight -- and looked like a surprised little owl.

'Oh!' Vawn said. 'Oh. Oh, how awful! It's that thing inside him! That bit of Shambles he swallowed! It's hurting him, it's disagreeing with him! Oh, what shall we do?'

'We'll shut up and get on,' Ispex said. 'That can't hurt Fang. He'll get rid of it sooner or later, one way or another. Where were we? A radio, yes.

They built a radio in here and talked at us through it. Right, how did they do it?'

'Dust,' Vawn said, uninterestedly. 'Their dust. I could smell it. It's obvious. Do you think his stomach looks swollen? I do. I'm sure it's swollen –'

Tsu said, 'Yes, dust. It must have been that. Intelligent dust. We already know there's dust here in *Starstormer* – '

'*Listening* to us,' Vawn said, dramatically, forgetting Fang for a moment. '*Spying* on us. *Eavesdropping* on everything we say.'

'All right, all right,' Makenzi said. 'That's enough high tragedy, Vawn. This radio of theirs . . . '

Shambles said, 'It's dust. I've worked it out. The antenna or aerial would be a con-connected trail of dust leading from here outwards and the receiver itself is no doubt a sim-sim-simple – '

Tsu said, 'I must fix his stutter.'

Vawn said, 'Fang saw it. Fang destroyed it.'

'True,' Ispex said. 'Ab-so-lutely true. But how did he see it? I mean, cat's eyes aren't as good as human eyes in most ways – '

'He smelled it,' Vawn said. 'It's obvious. Cats and dogs rely on their noses, they *smell* where things are. Then they *look*. Clever darling Fang – '

Ispex snorted, then said, 'Perhaps he did. But I don't think so. I mean, *we* could have smelled it out, that radio, if we'd wanted to. I mean, we could smell out the position of a bowl of flowers close in a dark room, couldn't we?'

'But we didn't think of it, we didn't try it,' Vawn said. 'Fang did, because that's the way cats

61

work. Nose first, then eyes. It's obvious.'

'No it's not,' Tsu said, over her shoulder. She was crouched over Shambles, doing things to his speech complex with a long thin screwdriver. 'It's not obvious to me, anyhow,' she said. 'Fang was looking, listening, sniffing, everything. And he was in a rage, a complete fury. He wasn't concentrating properly, and yet . . . Is that better, Shambles? Say, "ah".'

Shambles said, 'Ahhhhhh.' Tsu turned the screwdriver and the note of the 'ah' rose and fell. 'Try again,' she told the robot. 'Say your alphabet.'

'A, b, c, d, e, f, g-g-g . . . P-pardon.'

Tsu sighed. 'Shambles, I'm getting nowhere. Why don't you fix yourself? You can, you know you can.'

Shambles said, 'P-pardon, but I prefer not to.'

'He sounds a bit umpty,' Makenzi murmured to Ispex. 'Offended.'

Shambles must have heard Makenzi. 'P-pardon, but I am not umpty. Not in the least. So there.'

'Definitely umpty,' Ispex said. 'Oh, Lord. Wonder why?'

Again Shambles overheard. 'THAT CAT!' he squawked, so loudly that his voice cracked and strings of lights flooded his sides. 'THAT CAT! It provokes and annoys me, deliberately! It p-pursues me and p-persecutes me and p-pounces on me! –'

Ispex said, 'We're all very sorry, Shambles. I'm sure no disrespect was intended by us.'

'But it tried to *eat* me!' the robot complained.

62

'Only a little bit of you,' Ispex said, reasonably. 'I mean, there was a slight accident, and you fell over, and something fell out and Fang ate it . . . ' He paused. A thought had struck him. 'Wait a minute! Shambles, if Fang's got that bit of you inside him – and if his inside is full of digestive acids and things – does that mean – '

'It means I am connected to Fang,' Shambles said. 'It is a connection that I do not welcome.'

'What's all this about?' Makenzi began – but Ispex cut him short. 'Can't you see? Just *think* . . . Shambles, that component Fang swallowed – what *was* it?'

'One of my most c-complex c-components,' the robot said, with dignified anger. 'A communication-linked sensor with an emotive conditioner. Fortunately I possess several.'

'Fortunately, Fang possesses *one*,' Ispex said, gravely. 'Very fortunately for us.'

The others pressed him to explain: but Ispex looked wise and would say no more.

# SMASH-UP

The Starstormers held a party to celebrate nothing in particular. The party was over; the mess was still there to be cleaned up. Makenzi and Vawn were doing this chore while Tsu and Ispex made the three-hourly check of the ship – its Navplan, Aircon, fuel levels, drives, TVs, course, Ecoputer, Recycler . . . the list seemed endless and endlessly boring. Things kept going wrong. It was rare to make a check that didn't reveal faults that could lead to disasters.

Tsu sighed and said, 'Shambles, stick a probe in the Ecoputer.' Shambles slid a silvery tentacle into a tiny socket in the Ecoputer, the machine that – with the Aircon – controlled the climate and atmosphere of *Starstormer*. Lights flashed along Shambles' side. Ispex crouched to read them.

'It's lagging,' he said at last. 'Lagging again. There! Did you hear that double bleep? It's trying to catch up with itself.'

Ispex glowered at Shambles' read-outs, bit his lip and did mental sums. 'It's the monitors,' he said. 'Perhaps if we got Shambles to monitor the monitors?'

Then the ship seemed to jump and he was lying on his side with Tsu sprawled over him and a deafening noise in his ears. 4

They scrambled and butted and blundered along the curved, snailshell corridor to the *pow* controls. The ship was tumbling. The shock of the blow from the attackers had thrown *Starstormer* out of its proper spin into a new one. It made everyone dizzy. They got to their feet and fell over again, cursing.

Makenzi shouted, 'The TVs! There's no proper picture, everything's sliding! Vawn, get to the RV window!' But Vawn was hopping and yelping with pain, clutching her ankle, falling over, getting up again, her face twisted with pain –

A bellowing yell from an attacking craft, then the dying scream as it shot past –

Makenzi lurched drunkenly, unable to keep his balance, towards the RV window. Before he could reach it, there was another howl from an attacker and *Starstormer* lurched into an even worse spinning motion. Makenzi fell, heavily. On the floor, he said, peevishly, like a sulky infant, 'I'm *sick* of this!' – then pulled himself together, clambered to the window and stared out.

There was nothing new for him to see. Only luminous curves in the sky, the trails of the attackers: curves that swung away even as he watched because *Starstormer* was all wrong, dizzyingly wrong, gravity came and went, you kept falling –

Tsu shouted, 'OK, ready!' She had anchored herself to her *pow*-firing console with her legs. 'No, take the wobble plate!' Ispex shouted. She did not hear. Her face was no longer golden yellow, but putty-coloured. 'I'm going to be sick!' she shouted to Ispex. 'Hurry! Get the *pows* aimed before I'm sick – '

Ispex uselessly repeated, 'Take the wobble plate!' but it was useless. So he puffed and strained, trying to steady himself over the spin-wheel aimers. His head felt heavy. It wanted to loll and surge like a balloon. He felt idiotic and furious at his idiocy. 'Help me!' he shouted at Vawn.

'But the Navplan! – If I can sort that out, we'll be steady – ' Her face too was a strange colour, greeny-ashen.

'No, help *me*! Hold me steady, do the Navplan later! Help me!'

She tried to put a sort of wrestler's hold on his head and shoulders but was not strong enough. Still his head lolled uncontrollably. He had a flashing memory of a ride on an underground train – 'RECREATE THE PAST', that had been it, a school visit to a museum, and they'd all been taken for a ride in a quaint old twentieth-century underground railway train that swayed as it went along, and all the passengers swayed – that was what it was like. 'Use your feet!' he shouted. 'Lie down and use your feet!'

YEEOW-RAMMM! bellowed an attacker – then a slamming crash as a missile hit *Starstormer* and the whole ship shook. Vawn's feet were digging into his ribs, she'd braced her back against the curve of the wall and was trying to hold him steady with her legs and feet, it was working . . .

Ispex saw Tsu – why hadn't she gone to the wobble plate? – being sick into a bin, typical of her to find a bin, anyone else would have done it all over the console – and Makenzi on his hands and knees, shaking his head, he looked like a dog, what was wrong with him? – ah, blood coming from his head, he must have hit it on the wall – and the spinwheels felt funny under his fingertips, it was as if his fingers were numb, but never mind, here they come, get the symbols lined up – but was Tsu able to follow him, would she be able to push the firing tabs? . . .

Then, before the *pows* could be fired, came a terrible sound, a sound like the end of the world, a vast SMASH that shook and rattled and flung *Starstormer* right out of its horrible spin into an even worse one.

And there was light, violet light, flaring and flaming through the RV windows, ugly light, far too brilliant: and noises, explosions that seemed to swell in your head and fill it, pumping fog into it, hurting your ears, making your throat ache . . .

Why hadn't *Starstormer* burst, what was wrong with her? Why didn't she just burst into fragments of meteorite, shattered pieces of equipment, bits of people? Why weren't they all dead and done for and everything over at last?

The hideous light faded. Makenzi, his black hands patterned red with rivulets of his own blood, his eyes staring whitely, was prodding Shambles, trying to topple him back on his wheels. Vawn, on all fours, doggedly made her way to the Navplan. If she got there, the ship would be stabilised. Tsu stared at Ispex, her mouth working as she mouthed questions she could not hear.

But Ispex knew what the questions were. What had caused the vast explosion? Not *Starstormer*. The ship's *pows* had not been fired. So there could be only one answer.

'Collision!' Ispex yelled. 'The attackers collided! Hit each other! It must have been that! What else could it have been? Shambles, tell us! –'

Shambles whipped a metal tentacle into a display. The screen lit and showed brilliant green lines that recorded the tracks the attacking craft had made. The lines swooped gracefully. Then two lines met! . . . and still, on the screen, there showed the lingering, fiery trace representing the collision and explosion.

Makenzi, his wound forgotten, pranced and yelled. 'Smashed into each other!' he shouted. 'Ho ho! Smash-up! Smashed each other to bits! Your father was right, Ispex! – they're *not* infallible, not infallible at all! Ho ho!' He fell sideways, still laughing.

Ispex was not listening. Something in the back of his mind told his eyes to look for Fang. What was the cat doing?

There was Fang, over there! The creature had become a little demon, back arched, fur spiked and crackling with fury, mouth and teeth snarling, eyes blazing –

Fang was on the wobble plate. He was *riding* the wobble plate, as the oarsman of a dinghy rides his craft when he rows it standing upright. *Controlling* the wobble plate, throwing his weight, consciously, in the direction of the explosion.

And he knew what he was doing. Knew perfectly

68

well. Ispex could see that. The cat's energy, hatred, reflexes – his whole being – were in direct, conscious control of the wobble plate!

The noise of the explosion slowly died.

Vawn must have reached and recoded the Navplan, for *Starstormer* steadied.

Makenzi was on his feet, looking out of the RV window.

Tsu was again being sick, tidily and carefully.

Ispex stared at Fang, unable to believe what he had seen. As he stared, Fang changed. The little cat's eyes blinked and became mild. The arched back softened into a straighter line. The spine of prickled fur along his back flattened.

'Fang!' Ispex whispered hoarsely. 'Fang!'

The cat heard. He turned his head towards Ispex; blinked comfortably; lowered his hindquarters to a sitting position; wrapped his tail around himself; blinked again, and curled forward to lick the fine white fur of his waistcoat. He was still sitting on the wobble plate. He seemed quite at home there.

'*Ah!*' breathed Ispex. '*Aaah!*' Then he nodded his head three times; briskly but carefully removed Fang and set him down on the floor; then extended a podgy finger and touched the wobble plate. It wobbled. He stared at its unattractive battered surface. He smiled.

'I call a Council of War,' he said.

# COUNCIL OF WAR

'Council of war come to order,' he said, rather pompously. 'Now, listen. And think. Carefully. It's quite complicated . . .

'Fang hates Tyrannopolis. He hates the hot-metal smell. He hates the "flies" that Vawn used to moan about – '

'I don't moan about them!' Vawn objected. 'Not any more. I don't even notice them as much as I used to . . . '

'Fang does,' Ispex said. 'He notices them more than any of us, because he's a cat. Smells: they're *language* to him. And tiny things moving about, like the dust – they're his meat. Because he's a cat, a hunter. So – '

'Wait a minute,' Makenzi said. 'All that doesn't explain why he hates anything to do with Tyrannopolis. Get to that.'

'Oh, I thought you knew *that*. It's *obvious*,' Ispex said, smugly. The others knew that it *wasn't* obvious – that Ispex had thought long and hard. But they let him enjoy himself.

'It all started,' Ispex continued, 'with the bit of Shambles that Fang swallowed. Now, *think*: Shambles is programmed to dislike anything that may harm us, or himself, or the ship. Well, Fang swallowed a chip with that bit of the programme on it – '

'But you said Shambles *dislikes* enemies – yet then you say that Fang *hates* them,' Tsu said.

'Because Fang is a hunting animal. Wild, not rational. But Shambles is a machine, a rational being. Shambles *knows* we have enemies and does his best to fight them with us. But Fang feels *emotions* about enemies. He hates them.'

'And that was why he was on the wobble plate?' Makenzi said.

'Yes. He followed the signals – everything was connected up – and used his instincts and worked the wobble plate to try and get at the attackers. He wanted to kill them. But it was the bit of Shambles that he swallowed that made him able to – to sort of *feel* them: and the wobble plate let him sort of *see* them. Are you with me?'

Vawn and Makenzi looked puzzled. Tsu said, 'I see it all quite clearly. As you say, it's obvious.' (Ispex looked offended.) 'But what I want to know,' Tsu continued, 'is – so what? Fang sees and hates the attacking ships: so what? Who cares? Incidentally, has he been on his tray since the attack? Has he done his duty?'

'What's that got to do with anything?' Ispex roared. But then he said, 'Oh! I hadn't thought of that . . . '

'He did a big job soon after the attack,' Vawn said, fondly. 'Who's a clever boy, then?' she asked Fang, who blinked modestly.

'Did you put it down the Exall?' Ispex said. He was referring to the machine that got rid of *Starstormer*'s rubbish. Vawn said, 'No, not yet. Too busy. Why?'

Ispex said, 'If Fang got rid of that little pill he swallowed, he isn't any good to us any more.'

'Of course he is!' Vawn protested. 'He's booful!' She paused and said, 'Good to us for *what*?'

'Well, it's obvious!' Ispex said. 'As long as he's got that thing inside him, he's the most important member of the crew! Don't you see? – he's our *pow*-aimer! The perfect tracker and aimer! The hunter, the killer! I mean, you've all seen him chasing a bit of paper on a string, seen him pounce on that dust radio and destroy it! – you know how incredibly fast he is, much faster than any of us! – '

Tsu nodded gravely. Makenzi looked with new respect at Ispex. Vawn said, 'Wait a minute, I've just thought, perhaps I *did* flush the Exall – '

They all ran to the centre of the ship – and the Exall. Makenzi got there first. He lifted the lid and thrust a Glo into the Exall. 'All there,' he said, making a face. 'What a pong. Now what?'

Tsu said, 'Dial Rinse. Here, let me. Swill and rinse. And then we'll need a magnet. I'll bet there isn't one in the ship – '

'P-pardon,' Shambles said, and extended a metal whisker. 'Allow me.' He put the feeler into the Exall. The Starstormers waited breathlessly.

'I have what you are looking for,' Shambles said. He withdrew his feeler. Stuck to the end of it was a thing the size of a pea. The Starstormers let their breaths to in sighs of relief.

'With your permission,' Shambles said, 'I will take this component to the Char for washing and disinfecting; and then replace it in my person, where it belongs.'

'Oh no you won't!' Tsu said crisply – and snatched the little object from Shambles' magnetic grip. She hurried to the Char and quickly returned. 'Whose turn to feed Fang?' she said.

'Mine!' said Vawn. 'I'm sure it's my turn!'

'Stick this in his food,' Tsu said.

'Oh, but that's cruel! – '

'I'll feed Fang,' Makenzi said. 'Definitely. No argument. Where are you, Fang? Here, pussy-pussy!' He opened the fridge door.

Fang bounded in. He rubbed his head against Makenzi's ankles. 'Mrrps!' said the little cat. 'Mrraow!'

The Starstormers watched as Fang bolted his food, head jerking greedily. There were strangled purrs between gulps.

With one of the gulps, the programme chip from Shambles returned to Fang's inside: and Fang once again became the Master Hunter.

# CAT'S CRADLE

Later, Ispex said, 'It's still a Council of War. Places, everyone. We've got to talk about the wobble plate.'

'I thought Fang knew all about it,' Tsu said. 'He was using it. We all saw him.'

'No, he wasn't,' said Ispex. 'He was *trying* to use it: following the displays showing the attackers, shifting his weight so that the plate pointed at the signals . . . all that. But it's not good enough.' He blinked challengingly from face to face as if someone were to blame.

'Sorry, I'm sure,' Makenzi said. 'What *would* be good enough for Fang?'

'Revised wobble plate,' Ispex said. His face went pink with triumph. 'Got it all ready. Com-*plete*-ly revised. Here, catch hold, Tsu.'

He threw her a tangle of string. She caught it neatly and looked at it disdainfully, one eyebrow raised.

'What does Fang do with that?' Makenzi demanded. 'Learn knitting?'

Ispex did not condescend to reply. He started pulling at the strings, unravelling them. When he finished, he had what looked like a cage, or a hanging plant-holder – a round platform hanging from half a dozen cords. 'Very artistic,' Makenzi said, unenthusiastically.

Ispex frowned and produced the wobble plate and the circular display around it. This he fastened to the ceiling: then hung the string cage from it. 'There you are!' he beamed triumphantly.

Tsu was the first to make a comment, 'Have you gone mad, Ispex?' she said, in her high, bossy, clipped voice.

'But surely you see! – Oh, my mistake. I've left out the important bit . . . ' He dug in his pockets and came out with what looked like a ping-pong ball fixed to the end of one of Shambles' spare tentacles.

'Fang's target,' he said: and fixed this object so that it hung from the wobble plate. It dangled in the cage. It looked stupid.

'It goes up and down, it's sort of telescopic,' Ispex said proudly. 'It's out of Fang's reach when the enemy is too far away. It comes closer when the enemy's in range. And it swings from side to side, of course. Like this.' He tapped the ball. It bobbled.

Vawn said, 'You don't really think that Fang's going to have anything to do with that crazy contraption?'

'He'd better,' Ispex said. 'Anyhow, why not! I designed it for him!' But everyone could see the doubt on his face.

'Let's try him,' Makenzi said. 'Fang! Fang, where are you? Come and see what Ispex has *designed* for you . . . '

He found Fang and managed, after a struggle, to put the cat inside the mess of strings. Fang leapt out.

Makenzi re-inserted the cat and firmly pushed his furry bottom down on the circular base plate. 'Sit, Fang!'

Fang gave a high, pathetic meow and made a peevish attempt to scratch Makenzi.

'Show him the ball!' Ispex said, his face very red. 'It will be all right when he sees the ball! – and tries to catch it! . . . Like this, Fang, like this!' Ispex said, making the ball swing. 'Go on, Fang! Catch it!'

Fang looked at the joggling ball with terror. He tried simultaneously to hide from it and to back out of the cage of strings. In the end, he got badly entangled.

'Poor, darling Fang!' Vawn moaned, and ran away, clutching Fang to her neck. The Star-stormers heard her footsteps making for the centre of the ship, then a slam.

'She's locked herself in the loo,' Makenzi said. 'With Fang. Can't say I blame her.' Out of sympathy for the furious and baffled Ispex, he added, 'Well, that gadget of yours could have worked, I suppose. But I don't quite see how . . . '

Ispex explained, stiffly at first, until his enthusiasm ran away with him. 'The first wobble plate was designed for the human hand, not a cat's four paws and legs. So I redesigned the set-up. Turned it upside down. I gave Fang something to *chase*. Cats are supposed to chase things. Fang was being stupid . . .

'The other end of the stick is linked to the *pow* aimer and firer, through Shambles. Fang does it all – or *could* – faster than any of us could do it, because he's a cat. But he's also a stupid idiot, he won't understand. He won't *think*. I thought he'd enjoy it, look on it as a game . . . After all the fuss we make of him, and all the food we give him, you'd think he'd at least make some sort of *effort* – '

Vawn came in, flustered. 'Look, Mak, the loo won't flush and the Exall could be the cause, but the Exall's part of the Recycler and Ecouter so I think you and Ispex ought to have a look. I mean, if the loo won't flush – '

'Did you put Fang down it?' Ispex asked, hopefully.

'How could you say such a thing! The very idea! – '

'Just a joke,' Ispex said, bitterly.

And he and Makenzi went to find out why the loo wouldn't flush.

\* \* \*

They never got to it. There was a howling scream, a buffeting shock, a metallic explosion –

The attackers were back again.

'Why don't they leave us alone?' Vawn screamed. 'It was only a few hours ago that they – '

'Never mind that,' Makenzi yelled. 'Get to the Navplan. See if you can keep *Starstormer* on an even keel this time. If she starts spinning – '

'If only they'd leave us *alone*!' Vawn wailed, and ran to the Navplan.

Tsu, her golden face set, pushed and shoved at Ispex, who pushed and shoved back. 'Get to the

77

aimer!' she shouted. 'The old aimer! – never mind Fang's wobble plate – '

'But the wobble plate's better – '

Makenzi settled the argument by wrestling Ispex into place at the spinwheel aimer. 'Get on with it!' he shouted in Ispex's ear. 'They'll be back at any moment!'

He was wrong. The attackers went away. Tsu stood ready at the firing console: nothing happened. Ispex was poised over the *pow* aimer: there was no target. Yet Shambles told them the attackers were out there somewhere, quite close...

'Look!' Ispex whispered hoarsely. He nodded his head at the fifth Starstormer, Fang. The little cat was ablaze with fury. His body was rigid, his spiked fur seemed to crackle.

'He's smelled them,' Tsu said. 'The attackers! He's hating them!'

'Stupid idiot, he's looking the wrong way,' Ispex replied. 'What's the good of staring into the corner like that? They're not *there*! Look at the white ball, Fang!'

'Wait!' said Tsu. 'Wait! Look!'

In the corner, something formed. A mist, a spider's web, a cloud of flies... Fang spat and clawed. The cloudy structure kept on building.

A voice filled *Starstormer*, booming and flooding into every corner of the little ship.

'Are you hearing me?' the Voice said. 'Are you attending? Are you? Then hear what I have to say!'

'Tyrannopolis,' Vawn murmured. 'That cloudy thing's a radio. *Their* radio. We're hearing the

Voice of Tyrannopolis.' She brushed at the imaginary flies that tormented her. She twitched her nose at the smell of hot iron, growing stronger every moment. She began to whimper.

# FINAL WARNING

'Our destroyer craft are very near you,' the Voice said. 'Very near indeed. Already they have fired what you Earth people call a warning shot. I hope you are in a sensible frame of mind? I hope you can heed a warning? A warning from the Emperor himself?'

'Get on with it,' Makenzi said, huskily.

'The Emperor has instructions for you,' said the Voice. There was no humour in it now, no pretence of cool, amused pleasantness. 'The first is to return to Epsilon Cool and your parents. Immediately.'

'What happens if we obey? What happens to us when we get there?'

'You do the work he gives you to do,' said the Voice. 'You do it until you are adults and have given birth to children. Then you will be freed to do whatever you like, wherever you like.'

'No,' said Makenzi. 'We won't.'

'Then hear my warning,' the Voice said. Its loudness and certainty were terrifying. 'If you do not obey, your ship will be attacked, constantly, by our destroyers – '

'They're useless!' Ispex shouted. His face was scarlet. 'Crummy! They crash into each other! We'll smash them down, we've got weapons and aimers and – '

Tsu interrupted him. She told the Voice, 'You can't kill us, you know that. You can't afford to. You need us. So don't threaten to destroy *Starstormer*!'

'Listen,' said the Voice, louder than ever. 'Listen, *listen*, LISTEN! We will attack *Starstormer* whenever it takes any course not leading to Epsilon Cool. We will break your ship to pieces bit by bit. We will break *you* – your nerves, your resources, your will to fight – limb by limb, brain by brain . . .

'We will attack not only your ridiculous little ship, your *Starstormer*: but also Epsilon Cool. We will tear the settlement open. Destroy its covering, its ecodome. Your parents will die – '

'You need the parents as much as you need us,' Tsu said. As she spoke, she comforted Vawn, who was crying helplessly. 'Without us humans – '

'Without you, we are inconvenienced,' the Voice said. '*Inconvenienced*, no more. We want your hands, arms, muscles, eyes, skills. We need them. But the need is no longer serious. We now have Earthstyle weapons and ships. Now we can roam the Galaxy, hunting for any humans we may need, physically capturing them. Yes, the Emperor wants *you*: but there are other humans ready to be trapped and held and used . . .'

The Voice was silent for a moment. So were the Starstormers. They did not even look at each other. Only Fang was active. He sprang, snarling, at the cloudy structure of dust that was the Tyrannopolis radio. There was a soft thump as his paws alighted and the sound of his breath. The column shifted and swayed like a cloud of midges, unheeding and unharmed.

'Look at the cat!' said the Voice. 'Learn from him! See how furiously he fights – nothing: and gains – nothing. Learn from him! Learn to obey the Emperor! Obey!'

'No,' said Makenzi, his voice was tired. He looked from face to face, seeking support. Even Vawn looked up and nodded. 'No,' he said again.

'You have an hour,' said the Voice. 'Then the attacks begin. The attacks on you, that is: you and your amusing craft. Your parents can be left till later. Speak to them. Use our radio as well as your own. Ask their advice.'

'We know their advice,' said Makenzi.

'Speak to them,' said the Voice. 'Speak to them now.'

Suddenly the Voice was gone, and the thick welter of background pressure that accompanied it. And the Starstormers were alone, in silence.

\*     \*     \*

They tried to contact Epsilon Cool and their parents – and couldn't. The speakers howled and crackled and whined. No voices came.

Twice, the Starstormers thought they heard real signals – sounds from Epsilon Cool. But always, the meaningless noises took over, the noises from the space zoo, the howlings and twitterings and roars.

'It's no good.' Makenzi said at last. 'Not even with their radio boosting ours. Fifty minutes gone and no contact.'

The Starstormers, shoulders slumped, stood staring at the speakers.

Then Vawn said, 'I'm glad.'

The others stared at her.

'Yes, I'm glad!' she said. 'I don't want to talk to my parents. If we heard our parents speaking, we'd only go all . . . soft and stupid, you know what I mean. They'd tell us to save ourselves, and we'd say "Yes", and they'd agree to anything Tyrannopolis demanded, just to get us out of a mess . . .'

Makenzi thought for a moment and said, 'You're right. I don't want to be saved. I don't want to be killed, but I don't want to be saved.'

'Quite right,' Ispex said.

'All die happy,' Tsu said, mockingly.

'*I* will,' Vawn said, in a muffled voice.

'Our business, nobody else's,' Ispex mumbled.

Shambles said, 'P-pardon,' and blinked his lights.

'Well?' Ispex said.

'Nothing. Just p-pardon. I thought I detected . . . I may have been mistaken.'

'Detected *what*?' Ispex crouched to inspect the flashing read-outs on Shambles' sides. 'Look, if you think the attackers are coming back, make up your mind about it. And Tsu – we'll try Fang once more – '

'Don't be silly, he won't even go on the wobble plate, he'll just jump off! – '

'We'll use the old gear too. You and me as before – '

Shambles said, 'P-pardon' again, but before he could say more, the Voice of Tyrannopolis came through, filling *Starstormer* with harsh sound.

'The hour is up,' it said. 'Have you come to your decision?'

'Yes,' said Makenzi, grimly.

'Good. Excellent. You will alter *Starstormer*'s course at once and head for Epsilon Cool.'

'That's not our decision,' said Makenzi.

His voice was so choked that the Voice said, 'What? Speak up!'

'That's not our decision. Going to Epsilon Cool, I mean. We've decided to go somewhere else.'

'Where?' the Voice demanded.

'Anywhere the fancy takes us,' Tsu replied. Her voice was sharp, clear rude. 'Anywhere at all except Epsilon Cool. We won't be heading that way. Tell the Emperor for us, will you?'

'And while you're at it,' Makenzi interrupted. 'Tell him to take a running jump at himself on all eight of his octopus legs.'

The Voice said, 'You intend to be disobedient and impertinent? Very well –'

'Mind those destroyers of yours don't crash into each other,' Tsu said sweetly.

The Voice said harshly, 'Very well. Very well. Prepare yourselves.'

The Voice and its background sound were silent.

From the corner of the chamber where the Starstormers stood, there was a brief sound, a hissing rustle: the Tyrannopolis radio. They saw its dust gather itself together – rise in a spiral – then spread like mist as it hit the ceiling and rebounded. The mist began to fall, almost invisibly: but Vawn brushed at her face, feeling it, feeling the touch of the 'flies'. Her eyes widened with terror.

Then the terror was shrugged aside. Her hands were at her side, the fingers tightly clenched. 'Action stations,' she said, keeping her voice completely calm. 'Ho hum.' She rolled her eyes and pretended to yawn; then made her way to the centre of *Starstormer*.

'Good old Vawn,' Ispex said, almost to himself. Aloud, he asked Shambles, 'Anything coming this way?'

'No. I am sur-surprised.'

'You're sure they've nothing coming?'

'Quite sure.'

'Good. Come on Tsu, let's check out the old aim-and-fire set-up. And Mak, would you get Fang?'

'Why bother him? He's sleeping. Your Fang thing won't work, Ispex.' Nevertheless, Makenzi rumpled the little cat's body and said, 'Come on, rise and shine. You're going to fight the invaders. Or so Ispex says.'

Fang woke, stretched, sniffed and began to bristle. 'That's right, it's *them*,' Makenzi told him.

Shambles said, 'Pardon. I thinkinkink –'

'Well?' Makenzi said.

'A distant signal. Very d-distant –'

Fang sneezed: sneezed again; then bent forward and, with a modest air, coughed up the pill.

The little round object gleamed on the floor. Fang sat down by it, and regarded it without any particular interest. 'Oh, Fang!' Tsu shouted. 'For heaven's sake!'

Shambles said, 'P-pardon. Closer now. Five objects, possibly attackers.'

Ispex said, 'Do something, someone! Tsu, make him swallow his pill.'

Tsu ran to Fang and knelt beside him. She prised the cat's jaws open. 'Come on, Fang! Nice pill! Swallow it!'

He swallowed it, blinked, and spat it out.

Tsu groaned. 'Fang . . . please!'

Fang struggled, half-heartedly, and once again swallowed the pill. 'This time keep it down!' Tsu warned him. 'What is it, Shambles?'

'Speed of objects has increased. Estimated time of arrival now three minutes.'

Fang crossed his eyes and hiccuped. But the pill stayed inside him.

Makenzi said, 'I'll check the *pow* set-up. Never mind Fang, he was never any good – '

'Two minutes,' Shambles said. Now the display of lights on his side moved so fast and definitely that Ispex did not need to read them. 'They're almost here,' he said; and licked his lips.

One minute and forty-nine seconds passed. The attackers fired their first missile at *Starstormer*. Fang glared and spat – furiously. Ispex and Tsu crouched over their consoles –

And the battle began.

# THE LAST BATTLE

The first hit was a glancing blow. The Starstormers felt their ship shudder and lurch; and heard the ricochet as the projectile screamed away, twisting its own envelope of gases into a thin searing yell.

Ispex gritted his teeth and spun the aimer's spinwheels. Already, he was baffled and defeated. *Five* attackers. . .!

Tsu mouthed at him furiously, jabbing her fingers at the *pow* firing buttons. 'Why didn't you *aim*!' she shouted, furiously. 'If you don't *aim*, how can I *fire*?'

'Too fast for me,' he mumbled. 'Can't keep up –'

'What? What? They're coming *back*, find me a *target*! – '

SLAM! This time *Starstormer* shuddered and rocked. Ispex tried simultaneously to lock his legs round the pillar of the aiming console and spin the spinwheels. 'Hell!' he muttered. 'Hell, hell, hell!' The wheels blurred and overshot, he couldn't read them, couldn't keep up with their messages, couldn't control them . . .

'Fang!' he shouted. 'You stupid cat! Where are you?'

Above the noise and rocking Tsu mouthed furiously and Shambles flashed lights at him, meaningless lights. Ispex felt definitely and finally sick. It wasn't going to work. Nothing was going to work. The ship, the Starstormers and his own life were all come to an end.

Outside, there were yelling howls as the destroyers came in for the kill. And now Tsu was pointing, violently stabbing her finger towards the floor. She was shouting, Ispex could not hear, did not care –

Then he saw what she was pointing at. Fang.

The little cat's four paws were spread wide. Its legs were rigid. Its spine was tufted with raised fur, electric fur. Its jaws chittered. Its eyes blazed. It was staring upwards at the hanging cage, the wobble-plate cage: staring at the swinging white ball, wanting to get at it, capture it, tear it to pieces.

The ship shook and seemed to tumble. Ispex fell to his hands and knees. He had to crawl to reach Fang. He seized the rigid, vibrating body. Fang spat and clawed his hand. Ispex felt the sharp hooks tear his flesh, saw beads of blood jump out of the wounds.

The cat only saw the white ball.

Ispex lifted the cat and thrust it into the wobble-plate cage. Immediately, Fang scrabbled furiously to reach the only thing that mattered – the swinging white ball: the enemy.

'Connect!' Tsu shouted. 'Link him up!' Ispex did not hear. She had to do the job herself – disconnect Ispex's aimer, connect Fang's wobble plate, kick Shambles so that he too was in circuit. Ispex watched vaguely, sucking the blood from his scratched hand. His eyes were dull. He was thinking about death: his own death.

Fang, hind legs spread, reared up and struck out at the white ball. But the ball moved so fast, in so many directions. It teased him – jerked away, flashing and blurring, as it tried to follow the movements of five craft, each in different places, all travelling at insane speeds –

Ispex watched. It wasn't going to work. Five attackers were too many. He glanced at Tsu. She was biting her lip. She knew too, he could tell. Hopeless.

Fang, moving with impossible, furious speed, sprang upwards. Ispex caught a glimpse of white teeth, rigid tail, splayed legs, reaching claws – and the white ball swooping, the claws reaching – finding – holding –

And then all *Starstormer*'s energies were fed to the *pows* – and the little ship spat beams of pure energy – something exploded, big explosion – Ispex was flung sideways and hit the wall with his head – Shambles, upside down, paddling, his wheels turning, shouted, 'Hit! Hit!'

Ispex, dazed, shouted, 'We've been hit!' He reached for Tsu's hand, he had a crazy notion that he ought to shake hands with her before they both died, make a formal farewell –

'Don't *paw* me!' she yelled peevishly, pushing his hand away. 'Shambles, what do you mean, *hit*?'

'*Hit!*' Shambles squawked. 'Hit! Not *us*, not *us* –'

Blood trickled from Ispex's split eyebrow and blacked out his right eye. He rubbed the sticky stuff. The pain cleared his head. 'Who's hit what?' he said. 'Who's hit who?'

'Not *us* – *them*!' Shambles said. '*We* hit them!' Rivers of lights flooded his sides. The rivers steadied and held.

Ispex read the message the lights contained. 'We hit them. . .!' he murmured. '*We* hit *them*!' He began to laugh, shakily at first, then louder and louder.

Makenzi was there, crawling on hands and knees. 'What's happened, Shambles?'

'We seem to have hit two,' the robot said. 'One almost certainly destroyed – there are only four tracks left for me to follow. And one is flying a p-peculiar course, like a – like a – '

'Like *what*?'

'Like a b-bottle opener. No, that is not the word, p-pardon – '

'Oh, come *on*! – show us! On the screens!'

'There!' said Shambles. The screens showed bright curves that faded into nothing, three of them; and a faint distant glow ('The craft we destroyed!' Ispex muttered); and a fourth line, a spiralling line, still turning.

'Like a corkscrew,' whispered Tsu.

'Yes, p-pardon. Corkscrew. That is the word I was seeking.'

'It's still travelling,' Ispex said. 'I mean, the craft's still there. But out of control! Corkscrewing! We hit it, we hit it!' And now he was laughing again, bent double in a ball with his arms round his knees. 'We hit them! Tsu, it worked!'

She was not listening. She was staring at Fang's cage.

The little cat was like a wrestler in his ring.

The wrestler was stalking his opponent, moving in for the kill, closing in all the time, carefully but cunningly, crowding his opponent into the corner, making twitchy little threatening movements, snarling all the time . . .

Fang's enemy, the white ball, still moved. But now the destroyers were distant; so the ball was high, out of reach of the cat's ready claws. Tsu looked at the screens. They showed three lines coming together, almost meeting the corkscrew line. 'Look, Mak! Ispex, look! They're trying to do something about the damaged ship, I suppose. Straighten it out, get it going again –'

'Whatever it is, it's not working,' Makenzi said. The corkscrew line on the screen still turned and increased its spiral. 'That ship's had it!'

Tsu said, viciously, 'We ought to give it a final dose of *pows*. Why don't we?'

'Insufficient power build-up,' Shambles said. 'We must re-establish our energies. Will someone kindly place me the right way up . . . '

Vawn came in. She said, 'I was stuck there in the centre of the ship, nobody cares about me. We've hit one, haven't we?'

'One and a half,' Makenzi said, nodding at the screens. 'They can't get that other one back into action.'

'Fang did it,' Vawn said. 'Clever, darling Fang did it all. Didn't oo, darling?'

The darling spat, bristled and writhed its mouth ferociously.

'They'll be back,' Ispex said. 'Bet you anything. They won't give up.' He was gloomy again. 'My eye hurts like anything,' he said. 'I'm the only one that's injured. Look at my blood.'

The Starstormers watched as Shambles dressed Ispex's wound and Ispex complained. Now all of them were quiet.

'It's half-time,' Makenzi said at last. 'Score, one-and-a-half to nil. Let's have drinks and things.'

They raised their cups to Fang, their guard, sentinel, aimer and firer. Fang took no notice. He glared at the white ball, daring it to approach the curved claws and sharp white teeth.

Three of the four lines on the screen made lazy, distant, harmless patterns, centred on the fourth stationary dot, the damaged craft.

# ROUND TWO

'The lines!' Makenzi said, urgently. 'Look at the screens!'

The Starstormers looked: and without a word, got ready for action.

The lines were no longer moving vaguely. They had a purpose now. Three of them joined together in a tight pattern circling the damaged ship: then, as if giving it up as lost, exploded outwards – curving prettily, slowly, into separate courses ('Still a long way away,' Makenzi muttered) – and finally crept down the screen side by side, parallel. The dot of the fifth ship remained behind, fixed in space like a dull and fading star.

'Their course, Shambles?' Ispex said, over his shoulder. He was fiddling with Fang's cage. The cat watched him twitchily, resenting the disturbance.

Shambles flashed read-outs. Ispex glanced at them and said, 'Just what you'd expect.'

Makenzi said, 'What *do* we expect? Are they coming our way?'

'Of course. Going to have another bash at us. How long have we got, Shambles? Three minutes?'

'Two and a half.'

Ispex grumbled to himself and got on with his work on the cage.

Tsu said, 'Shambles, I'll stay at the firing buttons, but if Fang keeps going, I'll have an afternoon off . . . ' She pulled a face.

Vawn noticed that Tsu's fingers trembled; and felt her own mouth and nose twitch with a mixture of fear and hatred of the smell . . . the faint, but growing smell of hot metal . . . the smell of Tyrannopolis.

Makenzi said, 'I'm going to double-check the power levels and make sure the transfer from ship to *pow* is still OK. We could have burnt out something last time we fired . . . OK?' Ispex nodded. Makenzi left for the centre of the ship with Vawn.

Fang reached up his cage, standing on his hind legs, trying to sniff the white ball. He gave a complaining meow. The ball was still too far away to reach. But Ispex saw it had dropped an inch or more. He said, 'Connect and test, Shambles.'

Shambles slid out a snakelike tentacle. It neatly nosed its way into Fang's wobble-plate console. Another tentacle slipped into its socket on the firing console. He said, 'OK.'

Makenzi's voice came through. 'OK here in the centre. OK with Vawn too. You lot OK?'

They were about to answer when the first projectile, fired at very long range, hit *Starstormer*.

\*     \*     \*

The sound it made was almost a splash, instead of the usual SLAM. The ship rocked, taking the blow easily.

The Voice of Tyrannopolis invaded *Starstormer*'s

speakers. 'Warning shot,' it said. 'Obey the Emperor or be destroyed. Do you understand? Return to Epsilon Cool or die.'

Over the loudspeakers, from the centre of the ship, there came a rude noise. Makenzi had made it. The Starstormers heard him chuckle. They began to laugh. It was the wrong noise at the wrong time – a babyish reply to a deadly serious threat.

It occurred to Ispex that this could be the last sound Makenzi would ever make – his last word, his swan-song. He thought, 'What a swan-song!' He began to laugh.

He was still giggling as the screens filled with brilliant, blazing lines – and Fang, insane with rage, snarled and sprang at the bobbing white ball, close to him now – and Tsu's face was like Fang's, white teeth bared between twisted lips – and the Voice of Tyrannopolis, impossibly loud, shouted, 'HEAR! OBEY!'

There were tearing screams outside as the destroyers bellowed past. The screens were a mess of lights.

'WILL YOU OBEY?' The Starstormers yelled any words they could think of – curses and hoots and shouts of 'NO!'

The first missile hit *Starstormer*. There was no time for shock or fear or even pain as the little ship staggered and flung incandescent shards of meteorite – no time because Fang had pounced, and caught and briefly held the white ball –

The message went from him to Shambles, from Shambles to the firing console, from the console to the power transfer, from there to the darting sword of violet light that held, for a millisecond, one of the attacking craft –

All the power in *Starstormer* followed the hairline violet beam: followed and exploded when it found its target. Exploded, and burst the attacking ship apart.

There was no need to look at the screens. Light flooded *Starstormer*'s interior through the RV windows, flashlighting Tsu's rigid yellow mask of a face, and Fang in mid-leap, and Ispex's earnest face, eyes bulging with concentration, spectacles livid with reflected light, mouth a black hole.

And again Fang had captured the white ball. Again the violet beam probed and locked on. 'Fire! Fire!' Ispex screamed. Tsu jabbed ferociously at the *pow*-firing buttons, mumbling 'Fire! Fire! Why don't you –'

Shambles answered her. 'Recharge!' he croaked. 'Must leave an in-interval for recu-cu-cuperation –'

'How long do we wait?' Tsu shouted.

'Seconds,' Shambles answered. He was on his feet and wheels, anchored by his tentacles, flashing his lights. 'Any moment now . . .'

'Go on, Fang!' Ispex whispered. 'Go *on*! It's all yours!'

Mad with fury and hatred, the cat chased the white ball, bouncing its body off the sides of the cage, exploding like a firework in outbursts of crazed action –

'OK,' Shambles squawked. 'Recharged.'

'Go *on*, Fang! –'

Outside, a scream as a projectile hit *Starstormer* – but no SLAM, only the departing howl as the missile glanced off and spun into burning, exploding nothingness –

The white ball bobbed and jigged, following targets moving in different directions. Impossible to follow and hold them –

Yet Fang found and clawed the white ball for perhaps a hundredth of a second. The violet beam pierced the darkness of space – the pulse of enormous energy sped along the beam – and once again, *Starstormer* was flooded with livid fire, rocked by the blast of the explosion, spattered with flying, white-hot metal.

A kill or just a hit? No matter. The Starstormers cheered hoarsely and waited for the slow seconds to pass: for the power to build up.

Outside in space, something tumbled, a spinning mass of many-coloured fires, receding so fast that soon only the screens could show it. 'A kill!' Tsu and Ispex shouted, both at once.

And now one line, one line only, was left on the screens. Fang spat, clawed and yet again touched the white ball.

This time there was no direct hit. Yet the *pow* was close enough to be triggered. Its energy belched out in a great orange fog, a puffball that grew from nothing to everything faster than the mind could grasp it.

The screens flooded with orange: then with white and yellow. 'Hit!' Ispex yelled. 'Hit, hit, hit!'

'No!' Shambles squawked. 'Not a hit! – '

'But look, just look!' Ispex yelled. He was

dancing with pleasure, stumbling and capering like a puppet. 'Use your eyes!'

As he spoke, he shouted with terror and covered his own eyes. The puffball had grown grotesquely. Its brightness was hideous. The first white and yellow flare was joined by another forming a monstrous blinding explosion, impossible to watch even through the little R V windows.

One of the screens blew out its tube and exploded glass.

*Starstormer*, like a toy yacht suddenly caught in a vast wind, left her course and skittered sideways, driven by the blast of the explosion.

# LAST GASP

Tsu screamed and just in time wrapped her arms and legs round the stand of her console. 'My hair!' she cried; 'Don't! Don't! It hurts!' Her hair was blown forward, spiky and absurd. The blast was trying to pull it out.

Ispex, daring to open his eyes for a second, saw the sleeves of her tunic ripple and ruffle: then a seam split and, with a jerky slowness, the stitches came loose one by one as half of the sleeve ripped itself away and flew across the room.

'No!' he shouted. He knew what had happened. *Starstormer* had burst. The ship's atmosphere was exploding from her into space. He felt his mouth open and the skin of his cheeks tighten. It must be the dentist, he thought. Yes, the dentist. 'Open very wide . . . wider still . . . ' And the dentist's finger was pulling his mouth to one side, pulling hard, too hard, don't do that, it hurts! . . .

Then the dentist hit him with something heavy but soft: a big, soft club. He saw stars, then blackness, then nothing.

Tsu, clutching her head, saw him fall sideways. She had been hit too. Something, someone, had tried to pull her hair out and rip her clothes to pieces. Then came the big punch in the head. She reached out her bare arm towards Ispex, but then clung again to the stand of her console. She would be flung all over the place if she let go –

Something coiled itself round her chest and squeezed. She shouted with the pain. The staring whites of her eyes showed.

Then she too saw blackness, then nothing.

Shambles said, 'P-pardon. . .?' and painfully made his way, against the circular gale that had invaded the room, to the two bodies. He probed them gently. 'Excuse me,' he said, 'It's time to get up.'

Neither of them got up.

In his cage, Fang, mild-eyed now, tried to shake pain out of his head. He mewed protestingly: fought the pain: but at last gave in and fell over and lay still, with his mouth wide open and the small, perfect teeth showing.

*   *   *

In the very centre of the ship. Vawn and Makenzi felt but did not see the final explosion. They were flung against the wall – thrown to their hands and knees – left battered and bloody.

As they picked themselves up, the padded door of their tiny cell slammed shut, sealing them off. They felt nothing of the sucking blast as *Starstormer*'s atmosphere tornadoed through the hole in the ship.

'The others!' Vawn said. She sucked one of her knuckles. The skin was torn. 'What about the others? The speakers are dead.' The blood round her mouth gave her a clownish look as if she had put lipstick on clumsily.

'Got to get to them,' Makenzi said. Then – 'This door doesn't want to open. It's jammed. Help me. Pull.'

They pulled. The door opened slightly. As it opened, it released a whistling whoosh of escaping air. Makenzi knew at once what that meant. 'Trouble,' he said. 'The worst sort. Look, Vawn, don't follow me. Stay here. We're losing all our air, our atmosphere. Try and do something useful with the Aircon and Ecoputer.'

'But we can't *make* air! –' Vawn began. Makenzi was already gone and the door greedily sucked itself shut as he left.

Makenzi found Tsu and Ispex unconscious; Fang struggling to rise, shaking his head; and Shambles furiously busy. 'Unable to reach!' the robot squawked, scrabbling its stumpy legs and reaching out uselessly with silver tentacles. One pointed to an RV window. The armoured glass was intact but the framing had distorted and shifted. Between the frame and *Starstormer*'s hull, air screamed. Makenzi felt a pain in his chest, an agony in his ears and head. Very soon, he knew, the air would all be gone. Then the Starstormers would die.

'Can't reach!' Shambles repeated. 'And even if I could, I haven't sufficient manual power to bend the frame –'

'Never mind that,' Makenzi gasped. The pain was almost unbearable now. 'Do what I do, Shambles. Quick!'

He began tearing his own clothes, pulling his trousers off. Shambles, amazed, said: 'P-pardon!

The frame of the window is bent, we must mend the frame! – '

'Trousers!' Makenzi said hoarsely. 'Her trousers! And Ispex's! Get them off, quick!'

'P-pardon, but – '

'Quick!' Even as Makenzi spoke, he threw his jeans at the RV window. For seconds, they plugged the gap between frame and ship.

But then the material made itself smaller and smaller as if it were being wrung out. The trousers made a noise like 'GLUP!' – and disappeared into space.

'Hers! His!' Makenzi groaned, too weak now to help Shambles strip Ispex and Tsu. The Aircon moaned and whined, the Ecoputer flashed its panic lights. Vawn's voice, high with fear, came through the speakers. 'Look, I can't! – it won't – there's nothing for the Aircon to work on, or the Ecoputer! – '

Makenzi, his eyes almost starting from his head, twisted Tsu's jeans into a rope. He laboriously arranged the rope around the gap. The fabric drew itself into it, writhing, trying to escape. But it held. He took Ispex's trousers and completed the job. Now the gap was sealed: not perfectly, but well enough.

'C-clever,' Shambles said. 'Most ingenious.'

Makenzi, gasping, said, 'Help Vawn. Get to the Ecoputer. Aircon. Recycler. Anything you can think of. Burn fuel for oxygen, or something, I don't know . . . '

He fell forward on to his face. His black skin had

an ashy tinge to it now. His breathing was long, rattling groans.

Fang stirred. His flanks heaved. He let out a dismal meow.

The Aircon found something to get a grip on and made a very similar noise.

Makenzi muttered, 'Not dead yet.'

# VICTORY

Half an hour later, Tsu said, 'My ears aren't any better. In fact they're worse. Oh, my ears . . . '

' 'Ear, 'ear,' said Ispex. 'That's a joke,' he added, dismally. 'Get it?'

Makenzi said, 'Very amusing. If you'd just shut up for a moment, I want to listen to the Aircon.' He listened. 'Wheezing,' he said, 'Wheezing, but keeping going.'

'Like me,' Vawn said. 'It's not just my ears, it's my rib-cage, my lungs, my throat, everything.'

'You're alive,' Ispex pointed out.

'I know. That's the worst part.'

'At least you've got trousers,' Ispex grumbled.

'You'd be dead if Makenzi hadn't done what he did,' Tsu said. 'He created air. From trousers. Brilliant.'

' "His breath came in short pants",' Ispex said. 'There was a joke about that.'

'Oh, belt up,' Makenzi said gloomily. 'Who needs jokes?'

' "Belt up",' Ispex said. 'That's quite good, really. A trousers joke – '

Makenzi threw himself at Ispex and got him shoulders-down on the meteorite floor. Vawn watched with vague interest and tried to prevent Fang licking the blood on her wounded knuckle.

Tsu said, 'What's the course, Shambles? A28V on the grid?'

'A28V on the grid,' Shambles said. 'Spot on.' He flashed read-outs to prove it.

Makenzi, still kneeling on Ispex's shoulders, looked up and said 'A28V! Beautiful music! Bee-oootiful music!'

He began to sing it, loudly, disregarding Ispex's protests. 'Aye ... Two eight ... Vee!' Makenzi sang. 'Means all ... the world ... to meee!'

The others, all but Ispex, joined in, waving their arms above their heads, swaying their behinds, doing fancy steps with their naked legs. Even Fang, perhaps frightened by the noise, opened his mouth and mewed.

A28V on the Galactic grid meant Epsilon Cool. The Starstormers were on their way home.

# HOME

Vawn told her mother, Sheila, 'No, only once. We only heard from Tyrannopolis once on the way here. On the way home. It was funny, really . . . '

'They made their dust loudspeaker, you know,' Tsu interrupted, 'and the Voice came through, very loud and clear – I can't do the Voice, you do it, Mak –'

'THE EMPEROR COMMANDS!' Makenzi boomed, cupping his hands over his mouth to make a megaphone. 'THE EMPEROR COMMANDS INSTANT OBEDIENCE! IF YOU DISOBEY –'

'If we disobeyed,' Tsu interrupted, 'the Voice said we'd be attacked again –'

'And I asked, "What with?" ' Ispex said, beaming. 'And the Voice didn't know what to say to that. It shut up. Are there any more strawberries? I didn't know you could grow strawberries hy-dro-ponically . . . '

'Anyhow, the Voice went silent for a moment, having a think,' Vawn said, 'and then it said, "WE KNOW THE STATE OF YOUR SHIP. YOU ARE IN DEADLY DANGER". Which was true, it was only trousers keeping us going. Then the Voice said something about having to obey the Emperor and if we didn't we'd all die – all the usual stuff.'

She shrugged. Her mother shuddered.

'You're telling it all wrong,' Ispex said angrily. 'It was then I made my joke! You remember, Vawn! The Voice said, "I give you one minute to decide on your reply to the Emperor, and we were all a bit scared, because *Starstormer* wasn't going all that well, the Aircon was on the blink, and the trousers couldn't last for ever – and we were staring at the trousers, wondering if they'd hold out.'

' "THE MINUTE IS UP!" ' Makenzi interrupted, imitating the Voice. ' "WHAT IS YOUR REPLY?" – '

'And I looked at the trousers,' Ispex said, 'and I said – "Tell the Emperor to do what we did!" – '

' "AND WHAT WAS THAT?" ' Makenzi boomed in the voice of the Voice.

'Tell him to do what we did,' Ispex said. 'Tell him to stuff it!'

And for once, an Ispex joke got a laugh.

*Late in the night, when the only Starstormer still awake was Fang (who sat on the lap of Verona, Makenzi's mother), the parents talked.*

*'It's over,' said Clyde, Ispex's father. 'They're all asleep, safe as houses. So why do all of you torture your-selves by looking back at all the things that could have happened to our children? – '*

*'Did happen,' his wife Meg reminded him. 'Terrible things . . . '*

*'Yes, but it's over. They're here with us and we'll make sure they never leave us again. I mean, be sensible, Meg! Don't just sit there thinking of the past! Look forward to the future, here on Epsilon Cool! The future!'*

*Somewhere, a voice seemed to echo Clyde's words. 'The future . . . ' said the voice, very faint and remote. Meg stirred uneasily and turned her head. So did Vawn's mother, Sheila. But the others seemed to have heard nothing.*

*Jass, Makenzi's father, said, in his deep, slow voice, 'Roses. Strawberries. Wine . . . '*

*His wife Verona smiled. 'What are you talking about, you stupid man?'*

*Dexter, father of Vawn, said, 'Jass is right. I agree with him.'*

*'Agree with what?' Verona demanded.*

*'Roses, strawberries, wine,' her husband replied. 'We grow them now, today, here on Epsilon Cool, millions of*

kilons from the old home, Earth. And if we can do that now, just think what we'll be doing in the future! With our children beside us! Never mind the science bit, the hardware, the clever gadgets . . . The roses and strawberries and wine are real. Red and gold. The future . . . '
He smiled at first shyly, then enormously.

Again a small, distant voice seemed to echo the words just spoken. 'The future . . . ' said the voice. This time, everyone heard it and turned their heads to where it seemed to come from.

'The future,' said the Voice.

And then – 'THE FUTURE!' it boomed through the speakers. 'THE FUTURE! YOUR FUTURE? FOOLS! THERE IS NO FUTURE FOR YOU UNLESS YOU OBEY THE EMPEROR! OBEY, OBEY, OBEY!'

The Voice raved and raged. The humans, tense-faced, only half-listened. They knew what the words would be before they were spoken. 'OBEY! OBEY! OBEY!'

'Threats,' Jass said uneasily. 'More threats, new threats. I don't care about us, but the children are involved too. Do we tell them?'

'Of course not!' Verona said, sharply.

'THE EMPEROR INSISTS . . . ' shouted the Voice.

Above its din, Sheila said, 'No, of course not! They've had enough. They've fought and won their war –'

'Our war,' Dexter said. 'It was our battle they were fighting out there.'

'THE EMPEROR IS DISPLEASED!' the Voice hectored. 'THE EMPEROR WILL TAKE ACTION!'

109

'Keep them out of it,' Meg said. 'Let them enjoy themselves . . .'

In her mind's eye, she could see them, sleeping.

Tsu's face, secret and perfect, outwardly calm.

Makenzi, no doubt moving in his sleep, the strong black face glistening in the darkness.

Vawn, her face hidden by a thin white arm or a mane of hair.

And her own son's face, strange without its spectacles, but the lips stuck out as if they formed the word 'Think'.

'Let them sleep,' Meg said. 'Let them always wake happy.' She turned her head away so that her husband could not see the tears in her eyes.

The Voice of Tyrannopolis boomed on.

### THE END

The first two titles in the Starstormer Saga by Nicholas Fisk:

## STARSTORMERS

Makenzi, Vawn, Ispex and Tsu felt abandoned in their drab boarding school on Earth. How could they ever hope to join their parents, a thousand million miles away on Epsilon Cool? It was Makenzi who first said it (though Tsu pushed them into action) – *build* a spaceship! Together the children scoured the junkyards left over from the twentieth century and the result was *Starstormer*, a hollowed-out meteorite which, incredibly, proved spaceworthy. The Starstormers were launched on their first thrilling adventure...

## SUNBURST

In their second adventure alone in space, the Starstormers come across an immense abandoned spaceship, which appears to have come from Earth. Its field signal reads *Plague ship*! *Keep away*! But it may contain vital equipment, so the four children decide to go aboard. Once there, they discover the ghost ship's hideous secret – *too late*. For now *Starstormer* cannot escape the other ship's gravity pull ... and it is bound on a headlong course of self-destruction, destination – the sun!

## KNIGHT BOOKS